Into Dust

Kim Teilio

Into Dust
Kim Teilio

© 2023 Oxford eBooks Ltd.

Published under the sci-fi-cafe.com imprint.
www.oxford-ebooks.com

Illustrations by Catrina Parton

ISBN 978-1-910779-05-7 (Paperback)

sci-fi-cafe.com

PART 1

Chapter 1

THE CURTAINS, BEING of thin grey cotton, permitted the early morning light to enter the room with little resistance. Ryan Malin rolled onto his back, moved a hand across his face. He opened his eyes and saw the bottom of the budget-priced mattress suspended directly above him. In his peripheral vision, the red bars of the bunk bed frame. The room contained three more identical beds and two large wardrobes most likely sourced from a charity shop. Malin had been sure to book a night at the Holiday House Bed and Breakfast when it would be at its quietest and was more than relieved to have been the only guest.

It had been an entirely uneventful night in yet another place where guests regularly made mention of supernatural events on TripAdvisor.

He repositioned himself at the edge of the bed before sitting, the soles of his feet coming to rest on a threadbare carpet covered by alcohol stains. He had placed his neatly folded jeans and shirt on the nearest unclaimed bed, socks tucked into the brown boots he had slid under it. His military jacket, worn and now frayed at the wrist of the right sleeve, draped over the bars of the top bunk.

Malin slipped into his jeans and separated the curtains. It looked to be a dull grey morning in an entirely unremarkable seaside town. The street sloped downwards. Poorly maintained local businesses, properties and a train station between him and the uninviting sea. His visit here had been yet another waste of time. He was currently writing his eleventh book on his nights at supposedly haunted locations – it would have been long finished if it had not been for the whole Covid crisis – and the tenth was soon to be published. The books, and his fortnightly article in the local newspaper sold well enough to keep him from needing to find what his stepfather would have referred to as "real work". They sold exceptionally well each Christmas, for a reason he had never looked to explain. Financially, he was doing much better than most others of twenty-five years.

He finished dressing. The bathroom was located in the room across the hall. He stepped out onto the landing, listening for a moment and hearing nothing, before entering the bathroom. A motion detector brought the light on. The room was little more than a box of green tiles with an old toilet to one side and a cloudy mirror placed over a washbasin. Malin stared at his reflection. He had been meaning to shave his hair close to the scalp for a while now but hadn't quite found the motivation. The same could be said about his beard.

He splashed water over his face, urinated and returned to the guest room to collect his jacket and be sure he had gathered his other few belongings. It was 9.00 a.m. Had the owner not told him that she would wake him for breakfast at 8.30? It was possible that she had been distracted by other, more pressing tasks. It was just as possible, Malin thought, she regretted their introduction the previous afternoon.

"*The* Ryan Malin?" she blurted out, as she looked up

his reservation.

He nodded, "Um. Yes, that's me," he answered, narrowing his eyes, a little.

"Oh, I'm a big fan of your books Mr Malin," she said, handing him a key from one of the hooks behind the desk, "Though I never imagined you were —" she stopped herself, suddenly realising she was hurtling head-first into a terrible faux-pas. A painful couple of seconds passed.

"Black?" he offered.

The woman, flushed. "Sorry, I didn't mean to…" she faltered, "I didn't mean to offend."

Malin smiled politely. To be honest, he was pleased enough to be recognised, to even have a 'fan' to be put off by a clumsy turn of phrase. "Really, it's okay." He reached for the proffered keys, which the poor woman still held out for him.

The stairs groaned as he descended them, each individual step issuing a protest on having to support his weight. He remembered how one comment placed on TripAdvisor had suggested that – due to the vibrant colour and style of her hair–the proprietor would be the ideal candidate for the titular role, should a sitcom ever be made imagining "The retirement years of Ziggy Stardust."

A most unusual owner greeting new arrivals, a creaking staircase and the proximity of the sea meaning winds howled at the rattling windows. Combining any of these things with alcohol or an already active imagination was bound to encourage guests to imagine a peculiar atmosphere and lead to noises in the night appearing all the louder and without explanation.

Then there was the possibility that such places encouraged talk of unexplainable experiences as a form of publicity.

He smiled, recalling the time he had spent in York; of how a collection of pubs on a single street each had a sign of some kind on the premises upon which they claimed that *this* was the most haunted bar in the area.

Malin reached the foot of the stairs and turned into the foyer on the right. A large window above the entrance allowed plenty of light to bathe the area, encouraging the stairwell to appear much darker and narrower because of it. He found the owner at her desk, reading the morning edition of a local newspaper most likely shoved through letterboxes without charge, and smiled on having to acknowledge the resemblance to Ziggy Stardust all over again.

She became aware of his presence as he neared; looked to him with an expression that showed her surprise on seeing him. He knew it likely she had merely forgotten that he was still here but hoped even she had expected something more sinister, such as a ghostly apparition.

He considered asking her about her experiences here and decided against doing so just as suddenly. This was but another place to find its way onto a page in his notebook, a thick X beside it.

"Good morning," she said with a smile showing too many crooked teeth that had been stained by nicotine. "How was your night?"

He opted to tell her it had been *quiet*, as that was much more polite than saying it had been *disappointing*.

"We tend to get much more activity when the music festival is on," she laughed, taking the blue tin from the top drawer of her desk. "Students come from all over for it and their noise can lead to some… *disturbances*."

She handed him the £10 deposit that was to be returned when a guest handed back their key to the front door.

"There's a café on the corner," she said, remembering the offer of a cooked breakfast. "I can run down and get you something, if you'd like?"

"I'm fine, thanks."

She looked a little disappointed, the reason being that it was the morning breakfast run that usually guaranteed her a small tip. "Are you sure? They get deliveries from local farmers."

The world outside was cold and grey. Paint chosen for making front doors appear bright and vibrant looked muted. Malin began the walk towards the sea, each and every breath he exhaled forming a mist he then walked through. He tried to keep his surroundings from depressing him. The meaningless graffiti on boarded windows, the broken glass and crumbling remains of dog faeces on almost every corner was more than enough for him to know why this place was far from a successful holiday destination.

Apart from a lone dog walker dressed as if he were leaving for some Arctic expedition, the beach was deserted. Malin wandered the promenade, which he found to be just as lifeless, as cold winds felt to be clawing at his face. The flashing lights and overly loud dance music of the Penny Arcade summoned no custom. He was resigned to turning back and heading for the train station when he saw the sandwich board up ahead. Pink chalk against a black background stated:

What does your future hold?
EXPERIENCED palm reader
Only £5.00 for <u>unbelievable</u> accuracy!!!

He lowered his head and briskly walked to the sign that had caught his interest; was disappointed to see opening times on the door of the premises stating it would not be open for another half hour.

The whole trip looked to have been one massive waste of time and expenses.

He turned and made the uphill walk back to the train station, seeing only a few other people along the way. At the station he found the self-service machine was out of use and waited impatiently for a worker to appear at the service point. He took his ticket and his change without another word and made his way to the platform, where the train was already waiting.

Malin stepped aboard and found he had a carriage to himself. A newspaper had been left on the chair beside him – the previous day's but still something to provide a distraction. He scanned the pages, having no desire to read of minor celebrities or the patience for yet more government incompetence.

A shrill beeping sound preceded the doors sliding shut as the train was brought to life. A man's voice announced the destination and stopping points in between over the speakers, a static hiss audible in the background. He took a deep breath, quickly released it and tossed the abandoned newspaper to the vacant chair opposite.

He saw them on the platform as the train was steadily picking up speed, leaving the station falling behind. Despite the look of concern upon her face, Jemma looked as beautiful as he had always known her to be. Marie, now destined to remain but three years for all eternity, stood at her side.

Malin took his face in his hands and drew a deep breath, then another. He rubbed at his eyes before opening them, as if doing so would remove all sight of the woman and her young daughter. When he dared to look back out of the window, the station had fallen further back – the platform stood deserted.

Chapter 2

MALIN WAS MORE than happy with his chapter focusing on Holiday House within two days of writing. Having already researched the history of the property and the surrounding area before travelling there, he'd already had a rough – though workable – idea for the start of the chapter. Once that had been written, he merely had to incorporate the facts of his stay, the most important one being that he had experienced no supernatural phenomena or feelings of unease during his visit (he provided the loyal readers with such honesty). The chapter, however, ended with a mention of legends of witchcraft and how a palm reader now worked nearby. The area, he claimed, quite possibly acted as a magnet for the paranormal and could even be in possession of mysterious secrets.

He considered editing those final paragraphs. He wanted to remove the sense of the uncanny from the reader and provide them with brutal, unflinching honesty. He chose not to, for his readers did not seek such disappointment. They craved a secret, long overlooked knowledge, and he allowed the most gullible of them to believe that he provided. He felt, at times, that he encouraged stupidity.

No, not that harsh. Naivety. And there was a wide gulf that separated stupidity from naivety.

He was tired with reading over his own writing; sick to the back teeth with the name Holiday House and determined that this would be his final edit of the chapter when his mobile phone began to ring. The distraction comforted him and irritated him simultaneously. He looked to the screen and saw the Caller ID read: Joseph/Dad.

Joseph Hook was his stepfather and had been in his life for some fifteen years. His father – no, he consciously reminded himself, *biological* father and nothing more, Sidney Malin had disappeared from his life before he had lost the last of his milk teeth. As cruel and as cold as it sounded, Sidney Malin left for work one morning and simply never returned. Ryan's mother, a woman named Grace who was known for her beauty and her kindness, later revealed that she had received a cheque from Sidney a matter of months later, as well as an apology for leaving. She told him she had torn the cheque into pieces and set the letter alight.

Despite the years standing between now and such a fateful reveal, Ryan Malin occasionally found himself considering the contents of this letter. The burning ring of a gas stove could, without warning, bring all memory of the letter to mind.

He had asked Grace, long ago, what she could remember of the letter. She had told him that it had contained *self-pitying nonsense*, and how in her opinion, the paper that it had been written on had been worth more in value than the man.

Malin lifted his mobile from the desk and answered the call with a simple, "Hello." The sound of his own voice surprised him a little. He had been up and working for hours, yet he sounded as if he had just woken. The reason being, he was certain, that he hadn't yet spoken to anybody that day.

"Morning, chum," Joseph said by way of greeting. "You sound like you were writing until the early hours!"

"Mostly editing." Malin cleared his throat before asking, "How about you, are you working today?"

"No, I took today off, nothing exciting, just so there's someone here for the gas man to come and check the boiler. But what about you?" he joked, "How was your time at Hill House?"

"Not quite," Malin laughed. "It was quiet and nothing else. There are some interesting local legends, thankfully."

"Not a total waste of time, at least… I do have something to ask you, actually. You remember the girl I told you about? The girl I work with?"

Malin knew full well where the conversation was now headed. During the lockdowns caused by Covid, his three-year relationship with Amy Moers had come to a painful end. Combined with that, he had been certain the event had led to him having a mental breakdown of some kind. Though he was now, as far as he was willing to tell himself, over it all, he did not want another romantic relationship in the foreseeable future. Joseph, however, felt it best for Malin to find somebody else. Joseph was absolutely positive that the perfect soul to be this *somebody else* was a young woman named Karen, who happened to work in his office.

"Which one?" he asked despite knowing.

"Karen," Joseph said as if to remind him, "the girl I gave a couple of your books to?"

"You never told me you were having her read my books," he almost snapped back, finding himself somewhat ashamed over the idea of his work being scrutinized by someone he had never met.

"I'm sure I did. Well, anyway, she's really enjoying book six–"

"*Malin's Mysteries – The Trail of Dead.*"

"And she wanted to ask something about *The Long Cloak.*" Joseph claimed, "She really liked the story, and she wants to know if you think there is any chance it really exists?"

"I think we're safe to say it clearly doesn't," he responded coldly. "It's just another story, that's all."

"Well, she obviously enjoys how you tell them." Joseph answered immediately, clearly not wanting to be defeated. "But we all get paid at the end of the month and we're going for a couple of drinks after work. Maybe you could join us for one or two and talk to her about your inspirations and the strangest encounters you've experienced?"

"I think I've got somewhere else booked around then," he lied. "Some other time."

"Whenever you're free… Now, the other thing I've called about. It's coming up to your brother's thirty-third and me and your mother were wondering if you've any ideas how we can celebrate it?"

Chapter 3

MALIN HAD LIVED in his rented apartment for a little over five years. He neither liked the place nor disliked it. It was merely somewhere for him to live. A flat in an old Georgian building, a twenty-or-so minute walk from the city centre. It had been the property of one distinguished family until sold to developers who had turned the family home into a small number of individual spaces for professionals to occupy.

Malin resided on the second floor. The walls, ceilings and doors were painted white, the floors laminated, with the exception being the bathroom, where the floor was tiled. Those who visited occasionally claimed it would be so easy for him to make the flat appear much *nicer*, yet he had no real desire to do so. He had his bedroom, and he had his living room/study and that was more than enough space for him. How it looked was of no real importance, hence the windows that even he sometimes noticed were in need of cleaning. His only minor problem was that the central heating didn't function too well, but that was more than manageable when you lived on the top floor and therefore benefited to some extent from the neighbours below using their heating when it got too cold.

Sitting at his desk in the living room, gazing out onto the Georgian street beyond the sash window, he realised he had spent nearly fifteen minutes watching the world go by as he reflected on how long he had been in his home and if the time had come for him to move on, or at least do as others had suggested and decorate the place. He accepted that *this* was something of a coping mechanism. Something to be done whenever his brother was mentioned, more so if his brother were mentioned in the present tense, as if he were still here…

"Ian isn't here," he found himself muttering to himself, as if to convince himself. The unexpected sound of his own voice, regardless of how quiet it had been, surprised him.

But it was true. It was true every time he said it. Ian was dead, Jemma and Marie also.

In a moment of self-realisation, he accepted that two options were now available – to remain indoors with such thoughts and feel increasingly worse because of them, or to go out amongst other people and keep busy.

Malin took his laptop from the desk and shoved it into its carry case with newfound determination. He still had plenty of work to do before book eleven of *Malin's Mysteries* would be ready for his publisher and spending a little time in the independent coffee shop nearby could maybe even see him settle on a title, at long last. He checked he had his wallet and walked out into the communal hallway, the sound of his next-door neighbour's dog barking audible as he locked the front door. Looking out of the open window before making his way down the stairs, he saw a flock of seagulls scavenging in the middle of the road and he heard even more. The white Ford Transit parked nearby went unnoticed at this time.

Chapter 4

ORGANICO WAS A café in which Malin would always find himself feeling relaxed. A spacious, Victorian property, the glass front encouraged natural light to find every corner of the room, while the large and plentiful potted plants acted to keep the air cool. The glass front also permitted Malin, when he so desired, to simply sit and watch the people out on the high street. The staff were all moderately young and considered themselves to be *alternative*. The regulars were polite – many of them students from the nearby college or university and often kept themselves to themselves.

Malin stepped into the premises and smiled on seeing that although he may not have been the first to arrive and claim a space, plenty of tables remained for him to choose from. He approached the counter as one member of staff served a customer a large cappuccino and a slice of peanut cake to go as another replaced items missing from the refrigerator. It was this second member of staff wearing a tight-fitting Joy Division t-shirt with purple corduroy trousers who turned to Malin and granted him a friendly smile of acknowledgement. He smiled back at her, partly realising Taylor Swift could be heard playing softly over the speakers and yet this employee had not snobbishly decreed her to show her allegiance to the greatest post-punk group to come out from the north.

"What can I get you?" she smiled.

"I'll have a large latte," he smiled back at her, deciding regular milk would be good enough on this occasion, "with a three-cheese panini, please."

"Coming right up," she replied and quickly added, "I'll bring it over," before turning away from him. The staff member placed further along from her now free to serve the next waiting customer. Malin maintained his smile, turned and looked at his options, quickly selecting a free table against the wall to the left. He sat and removed his laptop, certain nobody would be looking at him, seeing him as someone longing for attention because he was deciding to work under their potential gaze. Not three years old and regularly updated, his laptop was soon open before him, and he had signed onto the secure WiFi provided for paying customers.

The café employee happily lowered his order down on the table as he glanced over his emails, which largely consisted of notifications for messages received over social media. He knew, from routine, he would have messages from dedicated readers both praising his work or suggesting a place to visit, as well as plenty of people angrily accusing him of taking advantage of a gullible readership. There was one, long overlooked email from his publisher, which he had been about to examine when he realised someone was standing before his table. He looked up and lost more than his breath; he felt the floor beneath him had been quickly swept out from under his feet.

She wore black Vans sneakers with blue jeans and a black t-shirt bearing a still image he recognised from a TV series streaming on Netflix; a navy-blue backpack over her left shoulder and then, he spotted, the small tattoo of an ancient rune of some kind upon the inside of her left forearm. Her light brown eyes managed to suit her strawberry-blonde hair without question; the frame of her oval spectacles so thin it was barely visible. She smiled, appearing a little embarrassed, before talking.

"I'm sorry, but aren't you Ryan Malin?"

Was he Ryan Malin? It was hard to tell. Just looking at her was enough for a part of him to doubt Darwin's Theory of Evolution. She was too beautiful to be descended of apes. This woman was surely of the angels.

"Yes," he smiled, her sense of embarrassment somewhat contagious, "can I help you?"

"I'm Kelley Stranack," she blushed. "I've tried contacting you on social media…"

Her hands moved as she talked. He noticed the reusable coffee cup she held. Written along one side was the question: 'What's the use?'

"A lot of people message me on social media," he said and immediately regretted it. Hoping it wasn't too late for him not to come across as supremely arrogant. He added, "It can take me a long time to go through them all… People often suggest places for me to look around; the occasional psychologist will want to ask me a few questions for a publication they're working on, or a radio host might want to interview me if something unusual makes it into the newspapers."

"I know you're bound to be busy," she smiled, somewhat apologetically, "but I was wondering if you would be able to help me with a little research."

He smiled, feeling at ease despite knowing there was every chance she would ask him something he had no knowledge of.

"I'll try," he said, bringing his latte to his mouth.

"I'm in the final year of my Masters at university, and my overly-ambitious dissertation is focusing on belief and it's also a study of mass hysteria and a lot of other things to try and cram into the word count," she laughed.

He smiled, nodded. "Okay," he said, "I think I'm with you… How can I help?"

"My lecturer has helped me gain access to an abandoned property, long believed to be cursed or haunted or both. I was wondering if you would be able to stay there with me and the lecturer for the weekend?"

For Malin, it was a most unexpected proposal. He knew his books sold, just as he knew they had claimed no academic praise. Could it be she merely wanted his participation in an attempt to have him viewed as the great charlatan?

"Me?" he asked, "What use could I be?"

She laughed a little before answering. It was a sweet laugh, impossible for him to believe she could be cruel enough to act against him in such a manner… He felt she laughed because – for her – he was unappreciative of his own worth.

"I've read each and every one of your collected stories, as well as the articles in the local paper. Do you want to know what I like about them? You're open, but you don't claim anything undeniably paranormal has occurred in your investigations," she went on without awaiting his response. "You'll talk of legend and rumour, but it's all there for people wanting to see it – you believe it's just another location claimed by rumours. But people still buy your books and choose to overlook what you've debunked… They like the idea that something *could* be there. Something that can't be explained."

Was she praising him or mocking him? He wasn't entirely sure.

"I wouldn't say I haven't found *anything* that couldn't be explained," he said, a little defensively.

"I know," she smiled. "You must have written a couple of hundred pieces and in a small number of them, you've described something of an unusual atmosphere. A faint knocking sound you couldn't explain. The others," she said, "are only too happy to jump on such things and exaggerate them."

A compliment or a complaint?

He smiled, shrugged and brought his latte to his mouth once again. "I just don't know if I'm the right person to help you with something so important."

She brought her backpack from her shoulder and opened it on the table, rummaging within until she had located a pocket-sized notepad and a pen.

"We're leaving at the end of the week," she said, scribbling away within the notepad, "and I would like you to at least consider joining us."

She tore the paper free, folded it in half and held it out for him to accept.

"You could even do a little writing of your own for your next volume of *Malin's Mysteries*, if you'd like."

Her eyes held onto his gaze until he blushed and had

to look away, fearful of confessing to her – or himself – that she was somebody he was certain it would be so easy to fall in love with.

"Free accommodation, free food, a ride there and back home. I'll even ask the uni' if there are any more funds available so we can *pay* for your time."

He laughed, looked to her and threw caution to the wind. He knew right away that he would be joining her and her lecturer, yet he took the piece of paper from her as if reluctant. "Let me see what I can find out about the place," he smiled, "and I'll get back to you. What's it called and where can I find it?"

She brought her backpack to her shoulder and smiled. "I've written it all down for you," she said.

"I'll let you know by tomorrow, at the latest."

"I hope you'll come. But either way, it was nice to meet you." She turned as if to walk away but paused, seemingly thinking better of it. "There is one more thing…"

"Oh?"

"There's a story in book four–" *Malin's Mysteries: Transformer.* "The place you were staying in had a moth infestation," she laughed.

"I know the one you mean." He nodded and grinned. "They were those, tiny, golden-brown moths."

"Yes," she said, "I can't stand them, neither. They always seem to flutter right at you and when you crush them, it's almost like they were made of dust."

"I feel exactly the same," he laughed, "or it's like they *turn* into dust – like vampires."

"I'll hopefully speak to you soon."

She turned and left without stopping or looking

back. Malin watched her through the window and, once she had left his sight, he opened the folded piece of paper she had left him and couldn't believe his eyes.

"You have got to be kidding…"

Beneath her name and contact details – Hewitson Cottage.

For a moment he could do no more than look at the name, prepared for the words to realise their error and to spell something entirely new.

He remembered trying, and failing, to arrange a visit to the grounds on various occasions. He would have gladly taken just a half hour! And he remembered how each and every time, he was told it could not happen.

And now, here he was…

Kelley Stranack, he decided, was surely an angel. No mere mortal could have achieved such a feat.

He was gulping down his latte and returning the laptop to its place within the carrier at record speed. Malin needed to return home, and quickly.

The black ring-binder had gathered some dust over the years. Malin took it from the top of the wardrobe, where he had intentionally been keeping it out of sight and pulled his fingers down the front cover to create four clear streaks.

His research folder on Hewitson Cottage.

He realised he was smiling, and that he was feeling *hopeful*. And, for him, it was with good reason. Access to Hewitson Cottage had always evaded him and now, now he looked to have been handed the keys to the kingdom! He had always felt this location had the potential to be a tome in its own right – not a small number of pages amongst a collection.

He opened the binder and looked to the most recent picture he had been able to locate; a single-storey, thatched roof cottage. A large window stood to the left and right of the front door, a much smaller window placed directly above it. Here, all windows and doors were kept behind sheets of iron that had been bolted and screwed into place. Signs plastered upon these warned of an unstable structure within, stated the property was a risk to life and – of course, trespassing was most certainly prohibited.

His hand trembled as he turned to the first page of actual research. A page on how Glenn Hewitson, a man of incredible wealth and influence, had purchased a nearby mine in 1900. Shortly after acquiring the successful mine, work began on the plot of land he had also purchased. Hewitson Cottage was to be his residence; he would move from London to be closer to his new business venture in the north of England.

Tragedy struck in 1903. On the very day the cottage was completed; the mine collapsed, and thirty widows were made. Hewitson remained in London and Hewitson Cottage was destined to remain empty.

Malin's mobile phone vibrated within his trouser pocket. He examined it, saw a message from Joseph/ Dad reading: Definitely on for something to eat after work on Friday if you're sure you don't want to come along?

Malin stared at the text for a matter of seconds, then thumbed a quick response. He told his stepfather he was too busy, that a dream study had been made possible at last and, feeling more committed to something than he ever had done previously, searched for the messages Kelley Stranack claimed to have sent to him via his social media profiles.

He found them instantly and assured her that he would very much like to go – if it were still possible.

Chapter 5

IT WASN'T A dream that night, but a long-forgotten memory returning to him.

He saw it as if it were happening in front of him. He saw it as it had happened, taken in by his eyes as they had been at some five years of age or less.

Malin hurried up the stairs, hands leading the way, as he acted as if he were a dog. He even felt the material of the old grey-blue carpet against the palm of his hands and between his small fingers.

He turned on the landing, paused, and sniffed at the air as if he really did possess heightened senses. Of course, he detected no scent out of place. He did, however, hear the voice of Sidney Malin, his strict-yet-loving father.

And, deciding it would be fun to creep up on his father as if he were a dog hunting its prey, he crept along the landing on all fours.

The door to his father's study was open, but only just. He caught sight of his parent, sitting in his office chair, holding a mobile phone to his ear that appeared so dated now yet was so advanced at the time.

"I'm being deadly serious," Sidney said down the line, "Marcus is going to have to–"

He swivelled around in his chair and momentarily looked to his son with wide eyes, as if he had been caught doing something entirely unjustifiable.

His eyes changed soon enough as he smiled, placed a hand over the mobile to keep what he was to next say between him and his son.

"Go get some ice cream from your mother," he quietly suggested, "and I'll be down in a minute."

Still smiling, he leaned forward, just enough to touch the door with his fingertips, and pushed it shut.

Malin woke. It was dark in his room, still the early hours of morning. He wondered why he had dreamed of that moment, of why it could possibly have been of any importance, and soon began to forget it. Soon, all that remained was a vague recollection of his father.

It was, he decided, of no importance, and so he stretched, intending to fall back into a deep sleep.

His foot brushed against something solid. Curious as to what it could possibly have been, he sat upright and, in the cold darkness, spotted the shape of a small child standing at the foot of his bed.

Marie.

His heart leaped to the back of his throat and froze. The silhouette remained still for only a fraction of a second and yet it lasted longer than any moment he had ever experienced before.

The shape turned and quickly rushed out through the open bedroom door, the sound of a child's feet running against the floorboards clearly audible, and silence returned just as suddenly.

He swallowed, reached out for the lamp on his bedside table and turned on the light. His eyelids instinctively brought themselves shut, but he insisted they open as much as they could. There was nothing to be seen but, believing he had seen – *heard* – somebody racing out of the door, he knew he shouldn't have expected to see anything out of the ordinary.

Malin removed the covers from his body and got out of bed, knowing he had to investigate.

Chapter 6

Everything was exactly as it should be. The front door was securely locked, as were the windows, and nothing had been disturbed. Malin had expected to find it as such, even as his heart was pounding as he had pulled the covers away to investigate.

He went into the bathroom and splashed cold water across his face, half expecting to see the transparent reflection of sweet Marie in the mirror when he had finished.

But of course, all he saw were his own solid features.

Had it all been a part of his dream, stumbling into the waking world alongside him? It was possible… He told himself it was more than possible, that it was most likely.

And hadn't this been *why* he had first started to look into the supernatural? To know once and for all whether he was truly being haunted by his sister-in-law and young niece, or whether he was losing his mind through grief?

He couldn't decide which possible explanation was worse; but he knew he needed to know more than anything else.

He was certain that, if he were to return to the bedroom, he would be asleep again in no time. It was this certainty, and the thought of troubling dreams that may soon find him, that encouraged him to make himself a cup of wild berry tea with honey… To sit with his laptop open before him.

Kelley was yet to reply to his response. He found himself a little saddened to think the whole investigation may have been cancelled for reasons he was still unaware of. Then he remembered how she was in her final year of study, and she was probably too busy reading and researching to regularly check her correspondence. In a bid to forget his reasons for being at his desk, he began to look over her own profiles on sites such as Twitter and Instagram.

She had shared a link to a song – *You're Gonna Come Around* by Matt Barton with Dave Owen and The Carers, and stated it should have been a summertime anthem. He saved the link and moved on.

She counted the Ramones, Dinosaur Jr, Mudhoney and The Finger as her favourite recording artists; she read William Burroughs and Brendan Mathews and her most-recommended book was Paul Auster's *New York Trilogy*.

She had liked a photograph and quote of Phil Spector.

Malin began to look through her photographs and smiled. Kelley Stranack was without a doubt the most beautiful woman he had ever encountered, and he was certain that she could be every song in the world to him.

He soon noticed how she was alone in every picture. Smiling to the camera on a beach or in a restaurant or on the campus library. Always smiling, always beautiful, yet never with a friend beside her. The photographer and the camera looking to be her only companion.

Malin envied the photographer. He wished it could

be *him* sharing each and every moment with her.

He smiled to himself, realised he was being foolish and tried to physically shake such notions from his head on closing his laptop. He drank his tea and turned out the lights, leaving the living room to return to the comfort of his bedroom.

He hadn't noticed the child's handprint in the condensation on the living room window.

Chapter 7

MALIN SLEPT UNTIL it was nearing midday, waking to the sound of rain hitting the outside of his windows. The air seemed unreasonably warm and he wondered if this was a sign of an impending thunderstorm. A part of him longed for thunder to finish the week. Thunder and fog were always handy to tell of an investigation where very little had occurred.

HE MADE HIMSELF a fruit smoothie with oat milk before running a lukewarm bath, which he simply lay in until the Nick Drake CD had finished playing on the micro-CD player in the living room. He hurriedly washed and dried; prepared a fresh cup of coffee with only the towel around his waist before taking it to his desk and going online.

Kelley had responded to one of his messages!

She told him how excited she was that he would be joining her on her study, and when he realised that she had included her mobile phone number, he allowed himself to believe – if for a single moment – that she had feelings *almost* as strong as his own. Kelley suggested they meet at Queensway Train Station at 10 a.m. on Friday morning (he immediately scribbled this onto his nearby desk calendar) before revealing her lecturer, Dr McNabb, would like to meet him for a conversation before they departed. She had included the good doctor's email address before signing off with a single kiss.

Why did the academically published professor wish

to speak with him, if not to later use what they had discussed in some great debunking of Malin's work?

He sighed; reminded himself of how he was something of the eternal pessimist before agreeing to meet at the train station at the given time. He then emailed Dr Rupert McNabb, to politely inform him he would be only too happy to make his acquaintance, before beginning a little research on the man. Surprisingly, what Malin found on him only acted to calm his nerves.

Dr Rupert McNabb taught, and extensively wrote on, Psychology and Religious Studies, but he also declared himself an expert in the field of Parapsychology and the Paranormal, Psychic Phenomena, the Supernatural and, last but by no means least, Witchcraft from the 1300s to Present Day. The man was also far from photogenic or stylish. The images available displayed him in light corduroy suits topped off with a beaten fedora hat, curls of light brown hair spilling out from underneath. Malin guessed the man's stubble was to try and have his face appear somewhat thinner, he looked to be sucking his cheeks in on any picture in which he was clean-shaven. When he smiled, he showed teeth which appeared far too big and too white for his mouth. They were almost regal in their appearance, resembling freshly cleaned tombstones of sparkling marble.

The pictures actively encouraged Malin to continue his research into the man. He uncovered that, in the early 1980s, many had predicted Rupert was exactly what the dusty, antiquated establishment was in dire need of – that he would draw in the best, most creative of minds. Rupert McNabb would be what the radical thinkers of the 1960s had hopefully predicted. Alas, it was not to be, and the man so many had wanted to believe in was soon on equal footing to the likes of David Icke or Uri Geller.

Still, Malin thought, it could be a wise investment, to have this man's opinions appear in the book he himself would now be able to write on Hewitson Cottage. As a matter of fact, Malin was more than confident that a number of his readers may already possess an interest in the beliefs of this man.

He realised his thoughts had led him down a worthless path; one which money was his key concern. He reminded himself that it wasn't – that it never had been. Had he not wanted to prove the existence of such uncanny experiences, if only to prove his own sanity? To *hopefully* find a way, a place, to successfully communicate with restless spirits?

Malin closed his laptop and placed his face in his hands. He thought of Jemma and Marie, and of the last time he had seen them alive. And he thought of Ian Hook, the stepbrother he had loved and lost, and he remembered the last thing they had talked of together.

Chapter 8

MALIN LOOKED TO his wristwatch. He had agreed to meet Ian at the café for 11.00 a.m. and had himself arrived at five minutes to. It had since turned 11.35 a.m. and still there was no sign of his stepbrother.

He knew it must have been hard for Ian. His firstborn child had come into the world while he was stationed in Iraq. Ian may have been home now, may have walked out on the career in the armed forces altogether, but his daughter seemed reluctant to accept him. There was still no bond in place. Jemma had said Marie simply needed time; that it was funny for them both, suddenly having a man in the house with them.

But Malin felt there was something else. Ian had walked out on his college course to join the army. He had seen both Afghanistan and Iraq, but something hadn't been quite right with him – not for some time. And it wasn't just the newfound responsibility of having a young child; it was more than that.

He peered into his cup – empty, then rose from the table, making his way back to the counter. The young man on duty smiled, expecting him to politely hand over his empty cup before leaving.

"Could I have another coffee, please?"

"Of course," the man replied, a little surprised. "Another white coffee?"

"Please."

The barista took to preparing a fresh cup of coffee

in a new cup. Malin glanced back and spotted Ian crossing the street. He was wearing his military jacket. He had previously kept good care of it, but now the sleeve of the right arm was beginning to get a little frayed.

And it wasn't *just* the jacket, Malin had come to accept. Ian himself was letting himself go. Bags under his eyes only hinted at the lack of sleep. But surely that could be chalked down to Marie's inability to sleep through the night?

"Make that two, please," Malin asked.

Outside, a motorist sounded his horn because Ian had taken to crossing the street before it was his time to go. If Ian had heard the sound of the horn or the shout of the irate driver he chose not to acknowledge either. He walked into the café as if he were a zombie, glazed eyes locking onto his brother once he had crossed the threshold.

"I'm sitting over there," Malin said as he counted a handful of change. There wasn't a single other customer on the premises. The brothers could have claimed any table they desired.

Ian looked to the table his younger stepbrother had singled out, looked back to him, nodded his head, and approached the table, already shaking his jacket free from his frame. Malin thanked the employee, handed him the cost of two white coffees with a small tip and returned to his table. He found himself a little irritated that Ian had taken his chair. He hadn't only sat there but was now draping his jacket over its back.

"I've got you a coffee," he said taking another seat at the table. Looking at Ian's reddened eyes and general look of exhaustion, he wondered if he should take it back and request a decaf.

Ian mumbled a thanks and scratched at an itch on his neck. Malin could hear the sound of his nails brushing against the thick stubble. Once, Ian had always been clean shaven. This close, it was even easier to see Ian wasn't quite right. He was on edge; his eyes moving from corner to corner, a sheen of perspiration was covering his forehead. It was possible, Malin reasoned, that his brother was coming down with a bug of some kind.

Ian reached for his drink and said, "It's too hot in here." The observation was almost enough for Malin to permit his mind to ease a little. Almost, but not quite.

"It's a little humid," he said in agreement. "We could do with some thunder; something to clear the air."

"No," Ian said, "thunder won't do it." and he brought his drink to his lips but then seemed to think better of it and placed the cup back down on the table. Malin noticed how his hands trembled.

"How are you doing?"

A part of him regretted asking the question before it was fully out of his mouth. It had been blurted out in a manner that could only show Ian how worried he was. The long game of slowly building up to the question could have been a lot better… Or so he had thought at the time.

"Don't worry about me," Ian smirked. "It's too late for me." He looked his young stepbrother in the eyes and asked him, "If something happened to me, you'd look out for Jemma and Marie, wouldn't you?"

And in an instant, Malin felt out of his depth and over his head.

"What do you mean if something happened to you?"

"If I couldn't be around," Ian said to clarify, "you'd look after them, wouldn't you?"

He swallowed. His throat clicked, loudly. The sound of passing traffic had vanished and, Malin thought, this wasn't a conversation they should be having here… Not where the bored employee could easily listen to what they had to say.

"You know I would," he said, "but I'd rather you were here with me."

Ian laughed and decided now was the time to drink a little of his coffee. "I'm marked," he chuckled without an ounce of humour, "finished. It's just a matter of waiting."

He wanted to make an excuse, any excuse, to leave the table. He wanted to text Joseph and have him come to them as fast as he possibly could. But before he could say anything, before he could even *think* of his next move Ian looked at him with those weary, broken eyes and continued.

"There was a tragedy out there," he spoke softly, "and I witnessed it and I guess I'm partly to blame because I didn't do anything to stop it, it just happened so fast but the jinn looked right at me, and I knew then it was over for me."

The word *jinn* was introduced to Malin's vocabulary right there. He foolishly told himself that a jinn was surely a respected scholar or figure of authority placed in Iraq. He could think of no other explanation for it. And he had wanted to reassure his stepbrother that he was back home now, and that the laws of his homeland would surely outweigh the judgements of a man in a distant country. In fact, he opened his mouth and was about to say as much, when his mobile phone started to ring. He smiled and said, "Hang on," intending to rid himself of the distraction with the press of a button.

The caller ID read Heather.

Sweet, promising Heather. They had known one another at high school and fate looked to have brought them back together. Whatever was transpiring between them could, in a little time, become a wonderful relationship. The flowers of their love were starting to blossom.

And he looked at her name and *knew* he should not answer at that moment; that he should contact her later that evening and apologise. But a small part of him considered answering her call, and Ian must have seen this confliction upon the face of his brother.

"I've got to make tracks," Ian said, getting to his feet and, already, he was heading to the door. "I'll call you in a day or two."

"Hold on," Malin had called after him, up on his feet with the phone still ringing, still vibrating, in his grip. He was still to notice that Ian had left his army jacket on the back of the chair.

"I'll give you a bell," Ian had insisted on stepping out onto the pavement. "Sorry for weirding you out."

And then he was out of sight. Heather was diverted to voicemail and Malin stood, the silenced phone in his hand, looking to the door his brother had walked out of. He noticed the coffee shop worker was now looking at him. He smiled, sighed, pushed the phone into his pocket and finally noticed the abandoned jacket. It was no matter, he assured himself. It gave him a reason to call Ian in a day or two.

He never saw Ian again. Not even a week after that final meeting, he was dead. A tragic road accident. His wife and child had been travelling with him.

And Malin was left to wonder, had Ian been too distracted to allow the road his full attention? Had he been too preoccupied with his other concerns, and could Malin have prevented the tragedy from happening?

He first saw Jemma and Marie on the day of the funeral and had put the sighting down to his unbearable feelings of guilt. But then he saw them again and again, and although he questioned his sanity, he was so sure that they were there, right in front of him. He was so sure they had something to tell him.

Chapter 9

MALIN ARRIVED AT the Costa Coffee in the heart of the city centre with ten minutes to go before he was to meet Dr McNabb. Barely beyond the entrance, he stopped and scanned the many people there. Young mothers and their babies meeting with family and friends; office workers on their lunch break, students and a lone patron here and there.

HE SPOTTED MCNABB sitting just to the side of the staircase leading to the first floor; a tabloid newspaper spread open in front of him. The man was dressed in a beige corduroy suit with a pale blue shirt and red cravat tie. The fedora he wore in the pictures Malin had seen was tilted slightly to one side. Malin took a deep breath, straightened his posture and released it on approaching the man's table, noticing the old brown satchel placed between his feet as he did so.

"Dr McNabb," he smiled warmly, "I'm–"

"Ryan Malin," McNabb finished, getting to his feet and extending his hand in greeting, "I'm very happy to meet you."

The two shook hands briefly then looked to one another for a moment, each waiting for the other to continue. McNabb decided quickly enough that he would.

"Call me Rupert," he insisted, "Dr McNabb is strictly for the book covers."

"I'll try and remember," Malin grinned. "Can I get you anything? Coffee?"

"Please," McNabb said delving into his pocket, "allow me to get these – it was my birthday recently, and someone got me a gift card that can be used here. What would you like?"

"That's very kind of you," Malin said, "I'll have the same as you."

"Shouldn't be too easy to forget," he laughed. "Please, sit down and I'll bring them back."

Malin thanked him and sat. He took a deep breath to steady his nerves – a feeling like he was attending a job interview of some form; hard to dispel. He glanced, fleetingly at the open newspaper. A reporter had written an article on a pet rat in Devon which supposedly picked the winning horses at the races. Malin smirked, looked away and took his mobile phone from his pocket. No missed calls or text messages received. He decided to scan his emails as he awaited McNabb's return; hoping, if he were to be honest, to see one from Kelley amongst the countless names he didn't recognise and the few that he did.

"I got you a cappuccino with a shortbread biscuit," McNabb said returning to the table with a tray in his hands. "I hope that's okay."

"Thank you," Malin smiled as he returned his mobile to the darkness of his pocket.

"Now," McNabb began as he took a cup from the tray, which he then pushed closer to Malin. "Let's get down to business, shall we? What do you think of ghosts?"

Now, more than ever, Malin really did feel as if he were at a job interview.

"Please," McNabb smiled before continuing in a tone

he had earlier selected, believing it made him sound as if he were deep in thought, "allow me to say just a few things first, so you are at ease and truly aware you are alongside a kindred spirit.

"Did you know," he asked, "that the instant a person is truly dead, they drop an amount of weight that scientists can't explain? A miniscule amount, really, but enough to register. The traditional eggheads," McNabb smirked, "are baffled. They've done all the tests and they simply can't say what it is that has caused the weight-loss to occur."

Malin nodded and pulled his shortbread biscuit from the wrapper before snapping it in half. "I've read some articles about that," he said. "Some people are saying it could be the soul leaving the body."

McNabb smiled. "You don't sound too convinced… Is the idea of the soul too outlandish for you? Consider this before you truly answer," he pleaded. "Respected, prize winning scientists all agree that Dark Matter is out there; that it holds everything together, across the universe. They simply can't see it," he laughed, "or truly explain what it is. Now tell me, would it be so far-fetched to state that Dark Matter is, in fact, God?"

"Science was never one of my best subjects."

"Nor mine." McNabb grinned. "Says a lot, doesn't it? The two of us were unable to grasp the cold and calculated explanations that are forced upon us, but we have excelled at thinking differently. We are leading figures in our own scientific field and I do believe that one day the term *paranormalist* will be just as admired as any other title in the field of science. Perhaps more so. Now you know where I have placed myself," he said, "I hope you can give me an honest answer of where you happen to fall on the topic of ghosts."

Malin bit into his biscuit and carefully weighed the words of his response before answering.

"I can't one hundred percent say that I have seen a ghost, but that doesn't mean I'm not open to their existence… Far from it… I just want to know that, without a shadow of a doubt, I have encountered a spirit. It sounds daft," he chuckled lightly, "but I feel if you could prove a haunting was taking place, you could possibly work out how to communicate with that spirit – if you found the right conditions.

"I want to know I'm talking with something from the beyond, and it isn't just my subconscious moving a glass around a board."

He knew right away that his answer had pleased Dr Rupert McNabb.

"I knew I was right about you," McNabb said proudly. "We almost met once, a few years back… We were both guest speakers at the Fake Truths Gathering."

Malin almost shuddered, recalling the Fake Truths Gathering. The organisers had booked the local library in a small city and invited a number of 'experts' to come and discuss the subject matter of their published works. He had found those attending to be desperate to believe in anything and everything that could not be proven.

"It was a busy event," Malin diplomatically chose to say.

"Maybe they'll hold another in honour of what you will write about Hewitson Cottage."

"I still can't believe we've been given access to the cottage," Malin said, shaking his head as if willing to be proven incorrect. "I tried a number of times over the years; I tried using the success of my books, my publisher contacted every name he could find and we were always turned down. How did the university manage to get us in?"

McNabb smiled, drank a little coffee to prolong his revealing the answer. "It's a privately owned property," he said at last, "and the university was willing to pay quite a sum."

"Three days, unsupervised," Malin remarked, "it must have been quite an offer."

"It was," McNabb chortled. "Money and the promise we won't bring charges against the owner should the place fall down on us!"

"I hadn't even thought of that."

"There's no need to," McNabb assured him. "We've already had someone go in there, and he reported the place as being in remarkable condition, all things considered. The cottage had been covered with signs warning of an unstable structure, but I've been told it's quite sound. Our man has been there this week, ensuring we have electricity and other comforts. The risk of legionella was, as you can probably imagine, a concern of the university."

"It is great to know you have someone seeing to things like this, but…"

"*But*?"

"It could be nothing," Malin smiled, "but he won't be disturbing the place too much, will he?"

"No items of importance will be moved, let alone

removed," McNabb smiled back at him. "I'm quite certain that our arrival will be as if we have travelled back in time."

"The man you have there," Malin asked, "has he told you much about the place?"

"He's been instructed not to," laughed McNabb. "Believe me when I say, if there happens to be a room filled entirely with antique dolls, I will see it and learn of it exactly as you do. In the interests of scientific study, we're all going into this quite blind."

The two continued to chat until a set alarm on McNabb's digital wristwatch sounded and he informed Malin that he had to hurry along. He was soon to be taking a lecture at the university. The two men shook hands and told one another that they would meet again, as planned, at Queensway Train Station on Friday morning.

"If you need to get in touch," McNabb informed him, "Kelley will be able to give you my contact details. Otherwise, simply get as much rest in as you can possibly manage. I'm sure you will need it!"

Chapter 10

HEWITSON COTTAGE REMAINED abandoned until May of 1912, when it became inhabited by Christopher Smith, alongside his wife Abigail (nee Palmer) and their young son, Simon. Born of an influential family, Christopher purchased the property with hopes that the country air would benefit the health of his young heir, who had been plagued by problems of the lungs. In mail sent to his grandfather, Christopher wrote:

> *The interior layout of the property is ill-thought out but can easily be remedied. The land has room for a few horses and Abigail has suggested a pond of some kind.*

> *Although a pond was completed, Christopher later wrote of his difficulties in finding men willing to renovate the property as local superstition had already spread throughout the nearest towns.*

In another letter, again addressed to his grandfather, Christopher wrote:

> *They talk of lights being seen from behind the windows throughout the years, as well as smoke coming from the chimney, and do not listen when I tell them this is impossible. It is, of course, a rumour most likely spread by poachers, who have taken advantage of the land being left unguarded for so long. Paying extra for the work of men from the nearest city is out of the question, of course.*

Abigail has suggested we approach the local vicar and request he perform a blessing of some variety, but I believe he would have to be granted permission from his superiors and that could take time I would rather not spend. It is, as I am sure you will understand, ever so tiresome.

Though Christopher continued to correspond with his grandfather, very few letters remain. One that does, dated August 1912 includes the following:

While it is expected for a child of Simon's age to have an imaginary friend, I do wish Abigail would not encourage him so. I feel as if I have been forced to watch a game unfold from the side lines, as the two make claims of time spent with visiting guests of whom I have been left unaware. I have told her to cease such childish behaviour, all to no avail. She merely looks upon me now with a mocking or, perhaps pitying, smile at her lips and walks away.

Christopher Smith returned to his family home in Oxford during the winter of 1912, following the tragic drowning of his wife and child in the very pond she had insisted upon. Despite many saying he carried a great sadness within him, Christopher Smith volunteered for duty at the start of the Great War.

He was reported as being killed on the front line in 1915. His remains have not yet been uncovered.

Chapter 11

MALIN STOOD CLOSE to the entrance of Queensway Train Station and kept his eyes on the approaching traffic as travellers walked out onto the street with their luggage or climbed out of vehicles that had parked nearby. His laptop was in the carry case over his right shoulder, the brown leather suitcase beside him held jeans, shirts, clean underwear and a few toiletries.

He was wearing a Ramones t-shirt he had purchased especially for Kelley to notice.

Despite lights alternating across a collection of junctions, it appeared as if there was a steady, never-ending flow of traffic moving along the road. As the white Ford Transit van came closer, Malin thought nothing of it. Certain it would be joiners or construction workers travelling to a nearby site or supply yard, he even looked beyond it, looking farther back at the incoming tide of vehicles. It was only once the indicator light flickered and the vehicle dropped its speed and came towards the kerb that he focused on the windscreen and spotted Kelley behind the wheel. McNabb sat beside her in his usual corduroy attire finished with the old fedora. The two were talking and, once they knew Malin had been able to see them despite the glare of the sun against the windscreen, Kelley smiled and McNabb gave a friendly wave. Malin smiled, waved back and stepped forward. He intended to be in the van as quickly as possible, with

Kelley back on the road before oncoming drivers took to using their horns or complaining of how they were being held up.

As the van stopped near enough to the kerb, McNabb pushed the door open before he moved himself closer to Kelley's side, freeing up a little seat space.

"Morning." Malin smiled as he hopped into the vehicle. He tried to readjust his backpack into a position that would not prevent him from fastening his seatbelt, the suitcase already forced into the footwell.

Kelley glanced back at the traffic, quickly rotated the wheel as she pressed her foot down on the accelerator and within the blink of an eye, they were moving on. Truth be told, Malin was impressed at how easily it had come to her. He had failed his driving test on two separate occasions. The second attempt was even at the wheel of an automatic and he could respect most drivers despite his shame at giving up entirely, deciding he could travel easily enough on public transport.

"Sorry we're a couple of minutes late," Kelley said, "the traffic on Sothern Drive was terrible."

"It always is," he said, hoping to appear knowledgeable enough on the matter. And if she asked if he could drive? He would claim he lived close enough to the city centre to walk. He would even say that travelling the country by coach and train gave him the time he needed to write.

"Are you excited? I'm excited," McNabb said reaching forward to open the glovebox, "I've even made us a little compilation to listen to."

He pulled a CD in a clear case from the glovebox; lifted the CD from the case and pushed it into the van's CD player. The first song to begin was Donovan's *Season Of The Witch*.

"I'm excited," he repeated.

Chapter 12

FATHER BRANNEY HAD come to realise he could no longer ignore the rumours and speculation of Hewitson Cottage.

1915 had arrived and the bloody war had not ended. The numbers of reported deaths and casualties on European soil looked to be far greater than the number of new recruits to take their places, yet Hewitson Cottage remained the gravest concern for many a family.

Men still reported seeing lights from behind the glass windows. Others had heard childlike laughter coming from the woods nearby.

Christopher Smith, although dead, had been spotted waiting at the end of the road that one would take to reach the cottage. A strange automobile had been seen coming from this road at the dead of night, and it had left not a single mark upon the dust it had moved across.

For a time, the man of God had been certain that talk of the property was simply a way for people to forget their worry over patriotic friends and family serving out on the front line. He also knew without a doubt how the children still played on the supposedly haunted grounds. How evil could a place *really* be if the youngest of local children still went to play there, without fail, every weekend?

That was until the morning his maid, a young woman called Katherine Williams arrived to find him placed at the kitchen table, appearing pale and overcome with concern. Katherine had told others that she had pried as gently and as respectfully as she ever could and although the Father had revealed a little to her, he had remained as if far removed from her. She claimed he had told her of a dream that he had experienced the night before. A dream of Hewitson Cottage and the darkness it breathed out upon all those that ventured too close to its cursed grounds.

Father Branney had said something would have to be done about the building and its grounds but then he had smiled, as if realising for the first time how he was speaking to but a young woman, and he begged her pardon but told her he really did have to go to his reading room, and it was most important he be left undisturbed.

Katherine Williams had told everyone she encountered of what had been said – of how peculiar Father Branney had seemed. And although the people she told appeared to scoff at her account and assured her she was just falling victim to her own imagination, they were all greatly interested in what she had told them, and they told their own family and friends what she had told them and, each time, the story became that little bit more creative. When Sunday morning arrived, the pews were all claimed and there were even people standing near the rear of the church.

The good Father did not arrive to lead his sermon.

The gathered flock waited until a steady murmur became a collection of concerned voices.

When had Father Branney last been seen?

Some, not wanting to be potentially interviewed by officers of the law at a later date claimed the Father must have clearly forgotten to inform them he would be going away, and so the service had been cancelled. Others rushed to the small home he occupied near the church and, with use of Katherine Williams' keys to the property, ventured within.

Nothing had been taken. The residence appeared perfectly tidy and, more importantly, *secure*. Father Branney's belongings were exactly as one would have expected to find them.

But where was the Father?

One man decided the time had come to call the police whereas others, recalling what they had heard only too recently, made their way to Hewitson Cottage, arriving shortly before the first police officer.

The doors and windows of the cottage were all locked. The police officer, Balbenta, a young constable of Italian heritage peered through the windows and saw no sign of Father Branney.

Someone suggested he force the door open and many there agreed that it was the best course of action. Of course, Balbenta explained that he was unable to do so. The property was still *owned* by someone – though he wasn't entirely sure *whom* – and he was simply unwilling to damage the vacant home without being certain Father Branney was imprisoned within. And so, with much reluctance, the gathered curious made their departure as he assured them that Father Branney was sure to turn up soon, embarrassed by the commotion he had caused.

It was four days before a locksmith was called for.

He reached Hewitson Cottage to find Balbenta and another young officer awaiting his arrival. The police sergeant had known to keep what was to be done a secret, save people come far and wide to watch with ghoulish delight.

The air was understandably stale and the rooms dusty, but there was no sign of Father Branney. Balbenta almost sighed with relief. He was relieved, yes, but also a little disappointed. He had hoped the mystery of Branney's disappearance would be solved here, and now – that the man of God had died here, of natural causes, and returned to the loving embrace of his maker.

But it was not to be.

Under the watchful gaze of both officers, the locksmith secured the door they had entered through before the three men left. Balbenta looked over the property, certain he would not come here again, unless the local children took to vandalising the place.

The whereabouts of Father Branney would go unknown for many a year and, when the time did arrive for him to be found, Balbenta would be among those sent to investigate.

As he turned the key in the ignition of the patrol car, he had not a clue to what awaited him.

Chapter 13

THEY HAD BEEN travelling for a little over an hour, but Malin was already struggling to keep his eyes open. Travelling by road always caused him to fall asleep just as remaining awake while getting a haircut was also a chore for him.

He stared right ahead at the cars in front along the motorway and knew he would soon be sleeping if he wasn't provided with some form of break.

McNabb jerked forward, pressed a button on the CD player to bring *Witch Hunt* by Rush to an unexpected and premature end. Shaking his head and looking more than a little irritated, he shoved the little finger of his left hand into his ear canal and rotated his wrist back and forth.

"That whistling is getting right on my nerves," he said, exasperated.

Malin smiled and nodded. What whistling? He hadn't heard any whistling. Odd thing to say, but at least he had provided a small distraction to keep him awake a little longer.

A sign up ahead advertised a turnoff for a family restaurant. Malin thought of coffee, of stretching his legs and pointed it out.

"Should we have a lunch break?" he asked. "It's on me."

"The university will pay," McNabb said to him with an *almost* mocking smile; then he turned to Kelley. "What do you think?"

"I could do with a coffee," she replied, already gliding from one lane to the next.

Long ago, the restaurant had been a Little Chef. Despite now being Woolley's Waffles, it had maintained much of the original décor. Malin imagined the place as an Americanised spot of British soil; burgers with fries and a thick milkshake (or a Coca Cola) or waffles with fresh coffee. The drive-thru section saw a customer give their order before waiting for a server on roller skates to bring it over – roller skates? The party of three claimed a table that needed wiping clean. Malin didn't mind. He was finally sitting beside Kelley, McNabb facing them from his chair.

"Pretty expensive," McNabb observed as he looked over the laminated menu; spectacles he had taken from his jacket now halfway down his nose. "We're definitely going to have to keep a hold of the receipts…"

Kelley turned to face Malin, smiled warmly. "Seen anything?"

"Maybe the veggie burger," he said.

"Are you vegetarian?"

"Yes," he said. "I'd be vegan if I didn't like cheese so much."

Kelley laughed at the response and looked back to her menu. "I might have the beefburger… Just don't judge me."

"Already have," he joked.

McNabb's mobile phone vibrated in his trouser pocket. He took it in his hand, glanced at the screen and looked fleetingly in Malin's direction before focusing on Kelley. "Just had a message come through," he said, getting to his feet. "I'm going to give Marcus a quick call."

"Take your time," Kelley smiled.

Marcus.

Malin couldn't be sure why, but the name seemed familiar. Important, even. He watched as McNabb walked out the door with his phone pressed to his ear, trying, and failing, to remember when he had heard the name before… Only recently, surely…

"Are you okay?" Kelley said, "You look like you're in a world of your own."

"No," he assured her, "I mean, *yes*… I'm fine."

PART 2

Chapter 14

JAMES AND ESTHER Burrows stumbled upon Hewitson Cottage entirely by accident.

The two newlyweds were returning from their honeymoon when they decided to be rather spontaneous. They had been making good time on their journey; where would the harm be if they stopped in the country and took in the sights and saw how the country folk lived?

Quaint towns and sprawling farmland were picturesque for the two, having always lived in the rundown parts of claustrophobic cities. It's just that the two enjoyed the novelty a little too much and ventured a little too far.

The storm clouds appeared from nowhere, if not directly from a nightmare. In heavy rain that flooded the very ground they walked on; the lack of light made it near impossible for either of them to see.

They spotted the shape of the cottage in the darkness and excitedly rushed towards it. They pounded against the windows, the front door, for long, sodden minutes despite having accepted nobody was there even as they neared.

Esther suggested that the homeowner could be out, possibly at a farmer's market. It was James that suggested forcing their way inside. Esther had advised against doing so – though in the freezing cold and dark, she hadn't entirely meant it. As a matter of fact, she was quite happy when her beloved shattered a glass pane on the front door and reached in to open it.

The air was as if they had entered a long forgotten mausoleum, but at least they were out of the rain. That was what mattered most to Esther. James mused that the layout was *unique*, and not something you would likely encounter in the city. The property appeared tp be T shaped. A narrow corridor with two doors to the left and one to the right. The corridor opened onto a rather large, open kitchen. Tall windows in the kitchen had the falling rain sound as the fingertips of the needy and the ignored tapping at the glass in death.

There was no kitchen table, but there were enough drawers, mostly entirely empty, for James to rummage through until he at last discovered candles and a box of matches. Given the darkness of their surroundings, the light of the candle was almost blinding to begin with.

Esther was horrified at the dust. The property had been left undisturbed for so long, they had left footprints on the ground that looked almost as if they had been walking through snow. The worktops were just as filthy.

James had joked that they must surely be able to get the place for a good price. His joke had lightened the mood, yet Esther had still made it clear that she would never want to return here, no matter how good a job he did of tidying up.

They traced their steps, James excitedly wanting to see behind the three closed doors. The two on the left revealed rather spacious, yet completely empty, rooms. The single door on the right had clearly been the master bedroom. James decided this made most sense, although this room was almost, but not quite, as empty as the previous two rooms.

There was a wooden chest in a corner of the room. James, maintaining his sense of wonder, had joked about forgotten treasure. In reality, the chest held nothing more than a bundle of dusty, moth-ravaged sheets.

He said he was right about there being treasure. James had said they could fold a couple of sheets into makeshift pillows, have one to lay on and a few left-over to cover them during the night.

Chapter 15

THE INCREASINGLY NARROW country roads had been in poor condition, but even they had come to an end some time ago. The road on which the white Ford Transit shook and bounced along had long been little more than a glorified ditch. Tall trees at either side may have kept the travellers continuously in the cool shade, yet the vehicle's suspension had become as good as useless.

Malin could more than handle the uneven, seemingly unforgiving track. For him, the small mercy had been when McNabb had *finally* decided to lower the brim of his fedora and slip into a silent sleep. Before closing his eyes for rest, the doctor had spent much time complaining again about the whistling sound he could hear – even going as far, at one point, to use Google to see if he had suddenly developed tinnitus.

The only drawback, Malin felt, was he had still been quite unable to speak freely with Kelley. He had wanted to try to start a conversation with her but had decided not to, believing he would have had to speak loudly for her to hear him clearly and doing so would most likely reawaken the already irritable McNabb. And so, they had driven in silence, all radio stations long since out of range.

Kelley hit the switch for the indicator to come on, slowed her speed and turned right onto an even narrow road that Malin had not even seen coming. This 'road' – if it could be considered such – ran a matter of yards before an iron gate, chained and securely padlocked shut appeared. Whatever this gate was attached to was hidden by thick undergrowth and vegetation but, beyond it, Malin could see a long gravel path with trees and other undisturbed greenery continuing at either side.

Kelley brought the van to a halt before the gate and nudged McNabb in the side. "Here we are," she said.

McNabb stirred, muttered something, and lifted the brim of his hat. The very sight of the gate had him at once wide awake. Sitting upright, he laughed gently and rubbed the sleep from his bleary eyes.

"Here we are, indeed." he grinned.

"How are we going to get through?" Malin asked, "Is someone meeting us?"

McNabb delved a hand into his pocket and retrieved a key, which he held for Malin to examine. "We've already got the key. Would you like to do the honours? Go on," he insisted, "take it – the key to the proverbial kingdom!"

Chapter 16

INSPECTOR BALBENTA COUGHED into his fist and looked towards Hewitson Cottage. The thatched roof could do with replacing. Other than that, the place looked almost exactly as he had remembered it.

Balbenta glanced back to the police car he had arrived in. A young officer sat at the wheel as he had been instructed to. In the back seat, James Burrows. He was still wet from the morning rain; stained with mud. Eyes reddened by tears or exhaustion or both.

Burrows had stumbled into the police station during the early hours of that morning. It had taken the officer manning the desk, with the assistance of two other officers on duty an hour before he had started to make even the slightest bit of sense such was his state of distress.

By foot, the station was over an hour away and that was taking the quickest route.

Burrows had blindly staggered and stumbled through flooded fields and quiet roads, seeing no one at all until he had almost fallen into the police station.

Balbenta took his first step towards the cottage, the early morning mist appearing to part for him as he did so. It felt as if the cottage were growing; emerging from the soil and the overgrown grass to tower over him.

He told himself that he was being silly. He remembered his wife, sitting at home. Sitting? No. She would be preparing a hearty lunch by now. Unless he called and stated different, Balbenta always returned home for lunch with his wife.

The door to the cottage was ajar, a glass pane broken, as he had known it would be. Balbenta pushed the door open. Shards of glass had already been pushed to the side when the door had been opened previously the night before or that very morning. Balbenta doubted it mattered. From where he was standing, he could already see the back door. It was wide open, as Burrows had told them he had found it. As Balbenta took his first steps down that narrow corridor, a gust of wind forced the front door shut.

He assured himself it was the wind, anyway.

The locked trapdoor in the kitchen had been demolished, leaving a gaping hole in the ground. The shovel that had been used to do this was now leaning against the wall, like the person responsible had simply decided to take a break from all his hard work.

Balbenta coughed again from the dust in the air and looked down into the darkness. He could see the first few steps of old, grey wood. He couldn't see what they led to. Despite knowing he would have to go down there, Balbenta was glad he was yet to see what awaited him within the impenetrable darkness. He took a breath and pulled the flashlight from his coat pocket.

Chapter 17

KELLEY DIDN'T TAKE the van over fifteen miles per hour along the gravel road, but the sound of stones striking the underneath of the car were as if they were travelling at great speed. The trees standing sentry at either side maintained the cool shade. Malin was overcome with excitemen and wanted to look to his side to see if McNabb or Kelley so clearly felt the same as him, but was unable to look anywhere but straight ahead.

Dazzling sunlight momentarily blinded him as the trees kept with them no more. Quickly, he raised a hand over his eyes and saw it for the first time.

Hewitson Cottage.

The thatched roof appeared to have been replaced in the time that stood between the capturing of the photograph he had found and coming here. Remarkably, although he *knew* it would have had to have been done already, the door and windows were no longer boarded. He found himself wanting to laugh, to cheer, as the gravel drive came to a gradual end some ten or eleven feet from the front door. Despite his wants, Malin maintained his composure. If Kelley and McNabb could appear so calm, he felt it important he also should.

McNabb, however, released an appreciative whistle as Kelley brought the van to a stop near the property.

"It doesn't look particularly imposing, does it?" McNabb said, "If you didn't know about its history, it would probably just look like any other isolated cottage."

"Any other isolated cottage with its own private grounds," Kelley said as she gently removed the keys from the ignition, "keeping it from public view."

Malin had no interest in whatever else the two could possibly have to discuss. He pushed the door open and hopped out of the van the moment he had unfastened his seatbelt. Later, he would consider his actions rude; leaving his backpack in a place that could keep McNabb from easily stepping out, but in the immediate moment he simply thought of nothing else.

At last, he permitted himself to quietly chuckle approaching the cottage. He noticed the circles bored into the wall around the windows and door, where tightened screws or bolts had held the boards in place. He delicately reached out, stroked one of these holes with his fingertip and found a chalky residue that implied they had only recently been removed.

Still smiling, he closed his eyes for a moment and stepped back to take in his surroundings in greater detail; realised how the cottage appeared to stand in a square of tall grass and weeds that looked to sway of their own accord, the perimeter guarded by yet more tall trees that kept everything bar the cottage and its immediate grounds hidden from them.

McNabb, perhaps to repay Malin for blocking his path with his backpack, may have given him the key to the gate, but he made a point of keeping the key to the cottage for himself. Malin looked to the doctor with wonder as he took the key from his pocket and pushed it into the lock, a grin revealing his large, almost unbelievable, teeth.

"It feels like somebody should say something," he said. "It feels like something should be said to mark this momentous occasion."

Malin swallowed with anticipation. He heard the door of the van slam shut as Kelley exited it, but he could not bring himself to look away from McNabb's hand as it turned the key. This was a day Malin had long ceased to believe could happen.

McNabb smiled, raised his head and took in a long breath of the country air, slowly pushing the door to the cottage open – neither wanting to rush nor spoil the moment. "To unknown pastures," he announced.

As she took backward steps from the Ford, Kelley thumbed through the contacts saved to her mobile phone. "I'm just going to make a call," she said, "just to let one or two people know we arrived safely."

If the two men had heard her, they didn't acknowledge what she had said. In fact, she just about managed to hear Malin saying that something didn't make sense to him as the two entered the cottage and fell out of sight.

Kelley didn't take it personally. In fact, she welcomed the distraction as she lifted the phone to her ear.

"It's Kelley Stranack," she said once her call had been answered, "patch me through to Marcus."

There was an audible *click* followed by three short beeps. Marcus came on the line.

"We're here," Kelley said, "Rupert and Malin have just walked inside."

In a voice that could easily have come from an

East-London market trader, he asked, "How does the paperback writer appear to you?"

"Excited," she said. "It's too early to know whether he has any of this father's talents."

"He fell for you being a student easily enough," Marcus said to remind her. "If we're lucky, he'll have his father's gifts, but don't forget these things can skip a generation or two."

"Out of all the places he has written about," Kelley said defensively, "he only seemed genuinely troubled at locations where we ourselves encountered difficulties. I'm willing to bet everything and anything that he will be useful for us."

"Keep a close eye on him," Marcus said, "I'm still thinking there must have been another way…"

"There wasn't," Kelley said glumly, "it asked for us to bring him, remember?"

"And we've brought him right to it… If things start to get too tricky for you to handle, get him straight out of there. Understand?"

"I understand," she assured him.

Chapter 18

FRED BURGESS WAS out the door before sunrise.

The morning air was cold enough to delve deep inside of his chest before he had reached his work van, and so he hawked up a batch of phlegm and spat towards the car of a neighbour in the habit of playing his music into the early hours most weekends. Fred didn't pause to see whether he had successfully hit the vehicle; he opened the door of his van, climbed in and slammed the door as loudly as he could manage.

The air inside of his van was even colder. Taking the diary with its faux-leather cover from the dashboard, he turned the key in the ignition and set to clearing the windows of condensation. The radio came to life. Simple Minds finished and the early morning news started soon enough. The lead story was that the US Military had bombed strategic locations across Afghanistan in response to the terrorist attack that had just taken place on September 11th.

"About time," Fred muttered to himself, He opened the diary and turned the pages until he arrived at the current date. He was due at the local nursery for 9 am. He remembered scheduling the appointment; remembered how one of the teachers had told him how the fuses kept blowing. He had remembered attending that nursery and remembered his son's first day there. He'd be amazed if the job didn't lead to him rewiring the entire building.

Fred smiled at the idea of a decent payday and,

satisfied the windows were now clear enough, was about to reverse onto the road when his mobile phone started to ring. Receiving a call this early was more than surprising, it was outright intrusive. He glanced back to his home and saw each and every light was off, meaning it couldn't be his wife calling to inform him he had forgotten something.

"Who in–" he began, taking the phone from his pocket. He didn't recognise the number. A part of him began to feel a little afraid. What if he hadn't quite done something right, and there had been a serious fire because of it? Or if somebody had been electrocuted because of him?

Fred swallowed, took a deep breath and decided to bite the bullet.

"Burgess Electrics," he said. To be disturbed at this hour, he certainly wasn't about to claim that this was a *good* morning.

"Hi," a woman spoke down the line. "Can I speak to Mr Fred Burgess?"

Okay, he was certain it wasn't a fire or electrocution. What else could it be? Unpaid taxes? Insurance due to expire?

"This is Fred Burgess," he responded.

"Hello," she said, and he realised that it was true – what he had been told. You really could hear a smile in someone's voice. "Mr Burgess, my employer is hoping you would be able to see to a very important, very large, job, and in good time. He's curious to know whether you would be willing to get all of the men in your employment working on this, to see it completed as soon as possible."

Fred began to suspect the local job centre was trying to find out how many men he had working for him who also claimed unemployment benefits.

"Well," he said, "that would depend on how much money your employer would be willing to pay up-front."

"That's understandable," she said, still smiling down the line. "Would it be possible for you to meet with one of my co-workers at some point today? I'm sure he will be able to give you more details on what the job is exactly, and discuss how much we would need to pay for your time."

He opened his mouth and slowly drew his breath. Alarm bells were ringing. He felt it could be a wise idea to claim he was too busy; that he had too many customers awaiting his expertise for the foreseeable. It understandably came as a surprise to him when he said yes, he could meet.

He had a place in mind; a small café only locals to the area knew of. Fred believed the morning traffic would make it difficult – no, impossible – for almost anyone else to reach there in time if he suggested they meet within the hour. And if they called him again? He would simply claim to be far too busy to waste any more of his time.

Chapter 19

MALIN FOLLOWED McNABB into Hewitson Cottage. Firstly, he noticed the wooden floor. It was dusty, yes, but he estimated only a month or so of dust at most. Was the cottage regularly cleaned, or had the man charged with guaranteeing the place was ready for the weekend also cleaning? Doing so may have been considerate, but Malin had longed for the place to be *truly* undisturbed. He had wanted cobwebs in the corners at the very least.

The second thing he noticed, and this was the most alarming for him, was the electrical socket on the wall.

"Hang on a minute," he said, "I thought the place had been left abandoned?"

McNabb turned to him, nodded. The look in his eyes made it clear to read he had no idea where any possible confusion could be coming from. "Yes," he said, "it has."

Malin pointed to the sockets on the wall. "Then when were these added? It doesn't make any sense," he said, "the place has been left abandoned, but somebody thought the place needed working electrics?"

McNabb smiled as if he was aware of something so plain to understand but still beyond the grasp of his new companion.

"Electrics were put in around twenty years ago," he smirked. "You didn't once wonder how we would manage to have access to hot water? There was a boiler added at the time," he announced, "along with top of the range water-pumps, I believe."

"Why go to so much trouble," Malin inquired, "if you're only going to leave the place standing empty?"

"That's the mystery, surely?" McNabb grinned and, once again, Malin became all too aware of the man's unsightly teeth. "Whatever transpired here in its most recent history must have been pretty spectacular for such costly renovations to be so willingly written off."

McNabb held his arms out, the palms of his hands against the walls at either side of him as if, like Samson, he would push until the very structure holding him could withstand his strength no longer.

The walls were entirely spotless. Immaculate paint. Not white, but close. A shade of white, or magnolia? Malin would have to be clear on any such details when it came to documenting events.

"What can you tell me about previous owners and visitors?" he asked.

"Nothing," McNabb smiled as if the answer were funny. "I know it's belonged to a very private, global business-of-sorts for around twenty years, but I can't provide you with a ledger detailing who has been here and when." He laughed and said, "Don't forget – the less we know, the harder it will be to fake any of our findings."

Malin nodded. It made sense and, if all went well, he could surely request such details once they had finished here.

The two men entered the wide kitchen. Malin looked to the solid wooden table and chairs – he was correct in assuming were new, then he noticed the trapdoor underneath it and, more importantly, how it was made of a different wood to that around it. McNabb briefly followed his gaze, then looked to him with an even wider smile and asked, "You know about the cellar?"

"James Burrows was said to have murdered his wife and thrown her down there," Malin said, "in 1933. Police found her, along with the remains of the long-missing Father Branney. Burrows had said an unknown figure had attacked them during the night," he concluded, "but the police found only two sets of footprints."

McNabb stroked at his chin and, leaning with his back against the wall, looked to the trapdoor as he spoke. "You look at any of the letters or articles written about this place, and you notice how they all mention the layout being *peculiar*." Still grinning, he looked to Malin and said, "You do know there was an outhouse in the back?"

"Yes," Malin nodded, "I'm aware of that."

"We're in the kitchen," McNabb said, "and the three rooms on the way in are bedrooms – or two bedrooms and a study, I don't know… I knew someone a couple of years ago and he hinted that the bathtub is in the cellar." He laughed. "That would be unexpected, wouldn't it? Especially when you consider how dark it must have been down there, with no electricity."

Taking much delight in his action, McNabb slowly reached for a light switch on the wall marked CELLAR.

"Of course," he said, "we can see what is *really* waiting down there, and we can do so without candlelight but with the aid of glorious technology."

His finger landed on the switch and, with Malin watching, was about to press down on it when Kelley interrupted their discussion.

"We *could* go straight into the cellar," she agreed, her arrival having gone so unnoticed it caused Malin to jump, "or we could get all of our things unpacked and look around the grounds before it gets too dark for us to see anything of interest."

McNabb laughed and removed his hand from the switch.

"That sounds like the wiser option," he said, "we don't have to go running into the main event… We have plenty of time for that."

"Let's go, then," she said turning back to the narrow corridor, "there's a lot of ground to see and I don't want you to be out there when it gets dark."

"As always," McNabb announced, "you are the wisest voice in the room," though he looked to Malin, and grinned as he first gave an exaggerated shrug of his shoulders before rolling his eyes upward.

Fred Burgess pushed the final morsel of his bacon and egg sandwich to the back of his mouth and sucked the salty grease from his fingertips before moving the plate away from him. A couple of postal workers and bus drivers had come by and ordered takeout, but other than that the café had remained empty. He pulled his cup of piping hot tea towards him, blew on its surface and downed a cautious mouthful. It was strong, as he had ordered, and but five minutes remained until he was due to meet someone here.

He smiled, certain he would walk out after a polite ten minutes, without seeing anyone else.

Because of this, he was surprised as another man

entered – sharply dressed, maybe in his early thirties. Cleanly shaven, his dark skin had a healthy glow about it that suggested he used some kind of expensive face cream daily. This was a man who clearly took pride in his appearance. Fred almost gave a visible sigh of relief as the fellow walked right by without giving him so much as a glance and ordered a small white coffee at the counter.

Fred relaxed all over again. This new arrival was too well dressed, too noticeable, to be working for the job centre or even the tax office. This new arrival, he reasoned, was probably on his way from a hotel he had booked for a business meeting.

The man paid for his coffee, thanked the waitress and turned. To Fred's surprise, he headed right towards him, smiling.

"Mr Burgess?" he inquired.

Fred almost choked on a mouthful of hot tea, then struggled, deciding how best to respond.

"You *are* Mr Burgess, aren't you?" the man asked, already sliding a chair out from beneath the table. "The Burgess Electrics van parked outside is something of a giveaway," he said, sitting. "Now, I believe my employer's secretary called you first thing this morning and you suggested meeting here. I'm not too early for you, am I?"

"No," Fred replied and to mask his nervousness, took his napkin from the side of his plate and dabbed at his pink lips. "Something about a big job, isn't it?"

"Yes," the man smiled, and he simply stared at the electrician for an uncomfortable moment before laughing. "I'm sorry," he said, "I must have woken up before my manners. My name is Sidney Malin," and saying that, he offered the man his hand.

"Fred Burgess," he said, accepting it, "as you already know," he joked, albeit weakly.

"Glad to make your acquaintance." Sidney smiled. For so early in the morning, Fred thought the man looked remarkably fresh. He was a man used to little sleep, he reasoned, and of taking care of business at all hours of the day or night.

"Now," Sidney asked him, "what details, if any, were you given?"

Fred shrugged his shoulders and drank a little more tea despite having no desire to do so. The man at his table insisted on looking right at him, at all times, and made Fred overly conscious of his every movement because of it.

"I didn't get any names," was all he found himself able to say.

"Well," Sidney laughed, "my employer's name is Marcus and, given the time you were called, I'm quite certain it would have been Lol you spoke to. Lol isn't her actual name," he included, still smiling, "it's something of a joke."

"Right…"

"Our exciting news – for us, anyway – is we have finally come into possession of a property we have had an interest in for a very long time, and we would like it renovated with all professionals given employment being strictly local."

"Professionals? How big a job is this?"

"All working together," Sidney estimated, "I can see no reason why this can't be done in a week – give or take. You and your men will see to the electrics," he explained, "plasterers will be recovering where you have had to make your own entry points. Plumbers will see to the plumbing," he laughed, "and there will be a couple of others to see the other, little things are done. Like clockwork."

"Sounds like a big place…"

"It isn't," Sidney laughed again. "You'll probably be forced to sit in one another's pockets, but the generous pay will hopefully make it all worthwhile."

Fred looked to the man and wondered if it was possible that he was part of some religious cult.

"What is it your company does, exactly?"

Sidney smiled and took a breath before answering the question. "Insurance," he said, "on a global scale."

Fred accepted the answer and nodded his head. "It's a local property, then?" he asked, listing a few potential locations to himself. "Where about is it?"

"Well, it has its own piece of land surrounding it," Sidney answered. "Hewitson Cottage."

"Hewitson Cottage? I heard that old, cursed place had fallen down years ago!"

"I can assure you it's standing," Sidney laughed. "and it's certainly old, but surely talk of curses is beneath grown men?"

Fred laughed this time. "I think your surveyor needs to take another look at the place," he grinned. "There's no electric in that place! This isn't a quick rewiring job or anything you'd need me for – far from it."

"Actually," Sidney revealed, leaning closer to Fred so he could continue somewhat conspiratorially, "quite a famous musician purchased the property in the seventies and paid a phenomenal sum to have electricity brought to the place… Only to decide he didn't really want to live there."

Fred swallowed. "Paul McCartney?" he asked. "My brother swears he saw him once…"

Sidney smiled, leaned closer and whispered. "I'm not at liberty to tell you who it was, but for the amount of money my employer is willing to pay you for this," he said, "you may as well be working for Macca."

Fred smiled, leaned back and looked into his cup of tea. "It's out in the middle of nowhere," he reasoned, "even for out here. What is it you're planning on doing with the place?"

Sidney shrugged, then leaned back himself. "Be useful for team-building exercises and retreats. I even have the honour of being the first to stay."

"That's quite an honour," Fred laughed and, to afford him a moment to consider all that had been discussed, he drank a little more of his tea. "I'll tell you what," he decided, "if you have the money, I have the manpower, and you and your business can do whatever it likes with Hewitson Cottage.

"Have one of your people send me an email," he concluded, getting to his feet, "I'll need the details on start dates and payment."

Fred checked his emails the following morning and was surprised to see he had received an email with the information he had requested shortly after leaving the café. The money being offered him was too much to ignore, just as it was too much to question, and so he and all the men working for him arrived at Hewitson Cottage early one morning the following week. As he had been told to expect, a small number of other, reputable building contractors arrived. When each and every man was required to sign a Non-Disclosure Agreement before setting foot in Hewitson Cottage, they each smirked to one another and put it down to the eccentricities of the wealthy few.

Some smirked, though others felt quite uncomfortable, on entering the property and learning that – during their time spent there – a priest would be reading aloud (and in Latin) from an ancient looking tome.

Chapter 20

His LAPTOP AND mobile phone, with chargers.

Two changes of clothes, including underwear.

His sleeping-bag.

One towel.

One bottle of shower gel.

His toothbrush and a travel-sized toothpaste.

A notepad and a pen.

His wallet.

Malin felt more than a little embarrassed at what he had decided to bring when the time came for them to unload the van.

He saw three inflatable mattresses, with mains pumps.

One combination microwave oven.

A mini fridge-freezer unit.

Shopping bags filled with perishables, as well as two chill-boxes.

They had even packed, along with disposable plates and cups, a kettle and a toasted sandwich maker.

Feeling not only potentially underprepared but concerned he could even look rather stupid to his companions, he immediately decided he would write a section in his notebook on how he liked to 'rough it' during his investigations, and McNabb and Kelley had presented him with a new and luxurious option which he had never before considered.

With a little luck, and his leaving the notebook in a tempting place, at least one of them would read what he intended to claim.

"One of these mattresses is for you," Kelley said to him, smiling softly as if she had read his mind.

And for a moment, he wondered if she may have done just that.

"You shouldn't have," he insisted, taking hold of a box, "I'm used to slumming it."

"Well," McNabb grinned, dragging the small fridge-freezer closer, "this isn't the Ritz, but you can have first pick of the rooms." He laughed toothily at that.

Malin, feeling all the more embarrassed, smirked and turned to Kelley. "Shouldn't you get first pick?"

"That's a little sexist," she said, stern-faced until she could not keep herself from laughing. "I'm sorry, I was pulling your leg. But take first pick," she insisted, "you're our guest, remember?"

Malin gazed back to Hewitson Cottage for a moment and considered his options. He tried to remember something, *anything*, that could be used to draw a particular room to him but found himself unable to do so.

Two rooms on the left, he reminded himself, and one on the right. It stood to reason that the large room on the right was the master bedroom and so, it was only right, to him, that Kelley have it.

"I'll take the first room on the left," he decided aloud. "Front bedroom."

"Wise choice," McNabb practically applauded, "I'm sure. Just to break a little bit of bad news to you, we have no curtains whatsoever, meaning you could be woken with the rising sun! But let's get our rooms set up," he said gleefully, "and then we can go for our first little wander about the grounds."

"What about the remaining rooms?" asked Kelley.

McNabb turned to her and smiled, "I thought that would be obvious! Seeing as I'm a modern man, I'll take the main room on the right," he laughed, "just to prove I haven't any outdated, even sexist notions, along the lines of you getting the biggest room, solely because you're the only female!"

Kelley shrugged as though without a care and said, "That's fine by me," which was enough for Malin to wonder if she really did have no complaint about it because she wanted to be placed closer to him, or whether she simply didn't care which of the rooms she stayed in.

The windows had been recently cleaned. As Malin stepped closer to the tall window in the room in which he would be sleeping for the next three nights, a floorboard moaned beneath his weight. He looked down at his foot and slowly lifted it, trying to commit to memory which one would be best avoided once darkness set in. Then he returned his attention to the window. The windowsill was a little dusty, but only by a matter of weeks. A dead fly, plump as a grape, had been left undisturbed. Malin stared at it for a moment, then raised his head to look over the gravel road they had dutifully followed through the trees.

Something immediately caught at the back of his throat.

It was Jemma and Marie. He saw the two of them standing close to the treeline; Marie pressed tightly against her mother's leg, reluctantly looking back to the cottage from over her shoulder. Jemma was looking right at him; frantically moving her arms in a gesture clearly begging he run forward to meet them.

"Are you ready?"

He almost leaped out of his skin and went as far as to place a hand on his chest, turning to see Kelley standing at the doorway. She at once apologised for disturbing him and he knew she was trying her best not to laugh, to even *smile*, at his reaction.

"If you've got everything the way you want it," Kelley said, "we can head out."

Malin blinked, turned away from her and looked back to the treeline.

There wasn't a soul to be seen.

He released a breath, turned and looked at the empty room with its cracked washbasin beneath a clouded mirror in one corner, to the inflated mattress to one side with his sleeping-bag on top of it, then to the backpack and laptop carrier nearby. Finally, he smiled at his few belongings and looked back to Kelley. "I think I'm ready," he said.

They left by the backdoor. The brightly coloured, plastic walls of the porta-loo standing a matter of feet away momentarily prevented them from noticing the darkness spreading through the clouds overhead.

Malin took a breath and asked, "Is that really what we're using?"

"Are you trying to convince me you have never been to a music festival?" McNabb laughed. "Where's your sense of adventure? I'll be pretending I'm back at Glastonbury!"

As a matter of fact, Malin had never attended a music festival, but he had no interest in explaining that to

McNabb. Just as he had no interest in explaining how there was bound to be a rats' nest somewhere in the tall grass, and the rats would certainly be drawn to the porta potty once it was put to use… *If* they didn't happen to be drawn to it already.

McNabb closed the door behind them and locked it using a key he slipped back into his coat pocket. Malin intended to ask if that was really necessary – locking the back door when they were so far removed from other signs of life, but Kelley had captured his attention asking about his writing.

"That surely can't be the worst toilet you have ever used," she almost laughed. "Some of the places you have written about had been left abandoned for longer than here!"

"True," he shrugged, "but they were all within walking distance of a public toilet, and I was booked into a decent hotel nearby."

McNabb chose to ignore what the two had been saying and simply pressed his fedora down onto his scalp. "Weatherman said it was most likely going to be a wet weekend," he said. "It looks like it's safe to say he called it."

The sky appeared to have disappeared the instant they left the tall grass behind and navigated between the trees.

Malin looked heavenward. A rooftop of long branches and full leaves, interwoven and knotted. Occasionally, a flicker of light shone briefly in the minimal space between.

He realised he was smiling and wondered which could be the most likely of reasons, the fresh air or the sight of nature claiming such dominance here. Lowering his gaze, he looked straight ahead to uneven, solid ground and wondered if nature could reclaim cities as it had done here, or whether man had crushed its spirit with his stone and glass.

Here, paths had been long hidden by fallen leaves, spongy moss and small plants hoping to expand. Exposed roots appearing as the dehydrated remains of great krakens emerged at random intervals, as if the very trees longed to break the legs of those wandering the grounds.

"You could easily get lost out here," he observed. "There's no landmark or noticeable change, it's like the trees just run on and on."

"Once the light is fading," McNabb agreed from up ahead, "you'd have no chance. Best we just keep going straight… Tomorrow, we can set out early – and with a compass," he laughed, though it was easy to hear he was beginning to lose his breath. The man had clearly grown accustomed to sitting behind a desk or riding the train out to nearby cities to deliver lectures at the cost of no longer venturing too far out in the field.

"Can you just imagine what it was like," Kelley inquired, trotting deftly over the roots and fallen branches, "for James and Esther Burrows to come walking through here in the dead of night and caught in a storm?"

Neither man had a chance to answer. There was a sound akin to a foot stepping down upon a thick blanket of undisturbed snow one second and the next, McNabb was on the ground. It happened so fast, Malin wondered if he really had witnessed the man fall or if he had simply imagined *how* it must have looked. He had definitely heard the man call out an obscenity, he was certain of that much.

"Rupert," Kelley asked, trying desperately, and almost succeeding, not to laugh, "what happened?"

She hurried to his side and placed her hands under his arms, helping him to his feet. Malin stood, knowing it would be near impossible not to laugh at the other man's misfortune if he dared move forward.

"I stood on something," McNabb responded angrily, moving from her touch as soon as he could support himself. Turning to look where he had last placed his foot, he continued, "If I've stepped in animal crap in these new boots, I'll–"

"That *is* unusual," Kelley said, filling the abrupt silence as she and McNabb looked to the same spot. Malin knew he had to move forward now, just to share this discovery with them.

"What is it?" he asked, stepping towards them until he finally shared the sight with them both. It may have been a crow, it may have just as easily been a raven, but now it was little more than exposed bones and ink black feathers. McNabb's smeared footprint could be seen in those very remains.

"Fox must have caught it," McNabb reasoned first.

Kelley looked to McNabb; arched an eyebrow and asked, "One of those foxes with an air rifle?"

Malin smirked at the display of sarcasm.

"Prove it was shot," McNabb insisted, clearly annoyed. "I've spent countless weekends in the country and watched as plenty of birds on the ground haven't noticed the fox coming up on them until it's too late."

Malin looked to the remains, then allowed his eyes to follow the trail of feathers leading onward. He knew they could have easily been distributed by the wind; he still couldn't help but feel someone had left a trail for them to follow.

"I think I've just felt a drop of rain," Kelley said, lifting her chin to look up at the canopy above. She sniffed the air and nodded to herself.

Malin looked towards her and asked, "You think it's time to head back?"

"Let's head back," answered McNabb, already turning to lead the way. "I've no plan to break my leg out here."

Chapter 21

Darkness claimed the surroundings at a speed Malin had never previously witnessed and although, with lights on, Hewitson Cottage managed to become somewhat homely, it was impossible not to notice the growing cold. Despite this, the trio managed to be in good spirits and the conversation flowed easily in the kitchen.

Using three disposable cups, Kelley made them each a hot coffee. McNabb used the combination microwave to prepare each of them a frozen, three-cheese panini. Having previously worked alone, Malin felt it could be an idea to bring company on his next investigation.

"It's amazing how quickly people accept their surroundings," McNabb grinned as he struggled to cut into his panini with the flimsy plastic cutlery. "Just look at us, laughing and joking when all the while we're sitting directly above a trapdoor that leads into the cellar where two dead bodies were found… one of them a confirmed murder victim."

"We can't afford to focus on such things," Kelley said as she offered a nonchalant shrug of the shoulders, "We have the land we have, and God isn't building anymore," she laughed. "You could choose any point on earth at random and it's going to be unlikely that no one had ever died there throughout the centuries. We might get new buildings but the land they are built on keeps its history."

McNabb nodded in understanding and looked

to Malin. "This reminds me of a conversation we had, when you and I first met," he said. "Kelley is right, of course. So many people have surely died on every piece of land, some in unimaginably cruel and horrendous ways, so why aren't we practically tripping over ghosts? Or at the very least," he smirked, "walking through them?"

Both McNabb and Kelley looked to him, awaiting his answer, and Malin felt the fraud because of it. He wondered if *this* was why they had brought him here, to show him how he couldn't answer their most basic of questions – how he wasn't nearly educated enough, to show him how he had never glanced across, let alone considered, the most basic of angles.

The brief flash of brilliant white light appeared to explode within a single pane of the kitchen window. Both Malin and Kelley quickly got to their feet and stared to where the distraction had momentarily appeared. McNabb, having had his back to the window, enthusiastically got to his feet, looked back and then to Kelley for an answer.

"What was it?" he asked as she hurried to the door.

"I think it was a camera flash," Malin answered for her, still unsure whether events currently unfolding were all part of a plan to highlight his supposed ignorance.

McNabb quickly reached for a cardboard box and rummaged within as Kelley unlocked the door. "Wait!" he insisted before finally lifting an individual flashlight for every one of them. "We won't see anything out there, take one of these before you break your necks!"

Malin snatched a flashlight from McNabb's possession without hesitation and bolted out of the door. If this was all just part of an act, part of a hoax to belittle him, he intended to uncover it sooner rather than later.

"Wait!" he heard Kelley call after him as he ventured out into utter darkness. The moon and stars had been hidden behind a thick blanket of clouds and the northern wind was colder than any he had ever experienced before.

Malin turned on the flashlight and swept from left to right but saw no signs of life. Of course, the grass was tall enough for anybody to find cover in easily enough, but he returned the beam of the light upon the porta-loo and quickly moved towards it, believing somebody could have quickly hidden inside or even behind it.

He yanked the door open and found the cabin empty. He raced around to the other side, ignoring both Kelley and McNabb as they rushed out of the cottage to join him. Kelley looked to him and, appearing more than a little alarmed, asked, "Anything?"

He looked back. What little of her he could see courtesy of the artificial light spilling out against the darkness was still entirely beautiful. He saw her concern and assured himself that, if this whole expedition was a setup of some kind, then she was surely no part of it.

But what if she were simply acting? He reminded himself that he didn't know her. She was physically beautiful in his eyes, and he hoped her personality were just as beautiful, but that didn't mean it would be.

"Nothing," he said, frustrated at this recent mystery as well as at doubting himself.

No. Malin was used to doubting himself, he was frustrated at doubting *her*.

McNabb took a deep breath and looked to his left, then to his right, then finally Malin. "What was it you saw, exactly?" he asked.

"It was a camera flash," Malin answered. "It couldn't have been anything else."

McNabb considered this before looking to the sky. "Could it have been a flash of lightning? It does look like it's going to bucket it down."

"No," Kelley said gazing out toward the inky depths of tree line, "I saw it, too. It was the flash of a camera."

McNabb nodded and nibbled at the side of his thumbnail before talking again. "Maybe some kid on a bike?" he suggested. "You might have caught a glimpse of a light on their handlebars."

"It was a camera flash," Malin insisted, "I know what I saw."

Impatiently, he looked around him and tried to think of where any potential intruder could have headed. Remembering a documentary of some kind, he recalled an expert in human behaviour claiming that when chased, a person will almost always instinctively head left. The same expert claimed police officers were in fact taught to expect a person they may be chasing to head left at the first opportunity.

"I'm taking a quick look for whoever is out here," Malin said, aiming the light of his torch against the ground as he started walking to his left.

"I'm coming with you," he heard Kelley announce from his back as she caught up with him.

"I guess I'll be looking over here, then," McNabb laughed. Neither one of them turned to see where he was headed.

Chapter 22

THICK VINES AND branches hidden in the grass occasionally attempted to hold Malin back, but Kelley continued walking for the trees slipping between young saplings like they were air.

Holding the torch firmly, Malin swept the light over the grass to either side, illuminating Kelley in the darkness. She paused for a moment, head tilted just as determined as he was to find something. Of course, he painfully reminded himself, she may have simply been doing this to fool him.

"I definitely saw a flash of light," he eventually said.

"I know, I saw it too, remember? It wasn't the light of a bike, and it wasn't a flash of thunder."

He smiled briefly to himself and nodded. "It's just the three of us," he asked, "isn't it? There's no one else, documenting this in any way?"

"No," she assured him, "it's just the three of us."

"Rupert wouldn't ask anybody to keep an eye on us, without telling you, would he?"

"No," she said, "he's taking this just as seriously as I am."

They stopped at the edge of the treeline and simply stood before it in silence for a moment. Malin shone the light of his torch as far as it would reach, before being interrupted by trees and other undergrowth.

Somewhere in the distance, a dog howled. Malin laughed at the sound. Kelley immediately joined him.

"Sounds ominous," she quipped.

"My brother was in the army," he said, still grinning, "and he told me about these exercises they would go on, way out into the country. He claimed you could smell the soap or deodorant worn by someone on the rival team from a good mile or so away, if the wind was blowing in the right direction. He said you could hear someone mumbling from far off, too, if it was quiet enough."

Kelley looked to him and, despite the darkness covering her face, Malin knew she was smiling.

"Are you saying the dog we heard is most likely miles from here and not waiting to ambush us in the woods?"

"I bloody hope it isn't!" he laughed.

Kelley looked back over her shoulder. "We can see the lights of the cottage from here," she said. "Maybe you will be okay, as long as we walk in as straight a line as we can."

"Sounds like a plan," he said and as he took his first step into the woods, a dead branch snapped under the weight of his foot.

Chapter 23

RUPERT MCNABB STOPPED at the edge of the trees and looked back, just in time to see Malin following Kelley into the woodland at his back. He sniggered to himself and muttered, "Love's young dream," to the breeze, and then he looked back to the trees immediately before him. Venturing on, in his opinion, would be entirely foolish. He had lost his footing in the woods during daylight, now he was expected to explore them in complete darkness? And for what, a flash of light he had not even witnessed!

A flash of light, he readily assured himself, that he would have logically explained within an instant if only he had seen it.

No, he decided, turning his back to the trees, he would not be venturing into the deep, dark woods under current conditions! He smiled to himself, walked slowly back into the tall grass. Let the young boy with the foolish look of adoration behind his eyes follow the girl; the wiser, older man would not be leaving this place with a limp!

McNabb took a deep breath and allowed the cool, country air to fill his lungs. It reinvigorated him at once. Directly ahead, the cottage. Still smiling to himself, he gradually began to head right, deeper into the grass and the weeds. He could no longer see the light of Malin's flashlight and he smiled again as he guessed it wouldn't be too long before they found themselves lost in the woods and with no other option than to call out for help.

His help.

They really were, he decided, two immature youngsters, rushing headfirst into the darkness.

Without warning, a simple fact slipped by his defences and drew blood.

Malin's books outsold his own. Malin was also, quite easily, the more prolific writer.

McNabb sneered as he tried to convince himself that it mattered little to him. His own titles had been selling in remarkable numbers while the young upstart was most likely struggling with toilet training!

And his next offering – his own book on Hewitson Cottage?

He wondered if he could release it on the day Malin were to release his own. Let the two go head-to-head, the numbers deciding which of the two men possessed the most talent! McNabb would see to it that the only books Malin would be selling in the future would be from behind a counter!

The sky transformed into an endless sea of purple. Open-mouthed, McNabb looked at the display in awe. Eyes transfixed, he watched the lightning as it appeared from nowhere and coursed across the sky.

There came a rolling sound of thunder and the heavens returned once more to an impenetrable shade of black.

The entire display, although it lasted only moments, had been beautiful. It had been nature at its finest.

McNabb walked on as if in a daze (and, perhaps, he was), eyes skyward as his very soul pleaded for another marvel to behold.

He moved a step forward and his foot found no solid ground. He felt cold water at his ankle. His foot was submerged in water so cold, he gave an involuntary gasp and shuddered.

And yet he could not remove his eyes from the heavens, nor could he stop himself from carrying on. Both feet were in freezing cold water now. Water that grew deeper with every step he took.

Water already rising up his shins, nearing the knees.

The air had also turned colder. It troubled his eyes, causing him to blink a tear.

No.

He knew it was *fear* that was bringing him to tears.

And that smell! How had it not registered until now? All-consuming, the stench was as if creation in all its entirety were rotting!

McNabb begged his body to stop venturing forward; yet his legs would not halt, and his eyes would not look anywhere but to the darkness that stared back at him.

It was the pond.

McNabb told himself that was all that had happened… He had stumbled blindly into the pond and now some state of shock had taken hold of his body and was moving him onward in an attempt to get out of the cold.

But it was bringing him further into it! The cold water had already risen above his chest and was at his throat, tears streaming down his face.

McNabb took a desperate breath of air and was consumed by the depths.

Chapter 24

THE COLD FELT to be running through his veins, and penetrating his bones. McNabb had never experienced anything like it; had never before experienced anything so all-consuming.

And now, how could it all appear so beautiful?

Everything was so calm here in the cold.

It did not matter how endless it seemed here. A part of him accepted that this could not be a simple pond he had come to be in, the endless darkness with miniscule lights shining from so far away. It felt as if he were deep in space, far from harm, with nothing but the cold and the silence and the darkness. The peaceful, silent darkness.

McNabb slowly released the air from his lungs, closed his eyes and allowed his chin to sink to his chest. There was nothing wrong, he decided, with remaining here.

And at first, the ringing sound was so easy to ignore.

He was certain it was but a passing sound. Certain it was something that could be ignored. Something that would —

A strong and powerful hand grabbed him by the scruff of his neck then dragged him upwards without ceremony. McNabb's eyes shot open. He tried to scream in pain and, for his troubles, brought in a mouthful of cold, stagnant water. He immediately began to choke and on every breath he attempted to make, he only dragged more foul water into his chest.

The stars had gone; the peace had been replaced by a piercing wail.

The intensity of the sound only increased as he found himself being pulled onto solid ground – the water itself he was being removed from becoming increasingly solid as he was hauled from it until eventually he found himself coughing and spluttering on hard ground.

Bone-dry, retching and clutching at his throat. The high-pitched whine felt like a knife running through his skull, red hot at the back of his eyes.

And the smell! That foul, rotten smell!

"Open your eyes," a voice commanded, "and know me, for I have known you. Open your eyes and know my bidding is to be done."

McNabb did not want to open his eyes. He wanted to cover them. He would rather have plucked them from their sockets, but his own body betrayed him.

McNabb opened his eyes and accepted that he was on the ground, out in the tall grass, and he was not alone. A tall figure stood over him. A tall figure in matted, stinking furs with a scythe akin to Death's own in its twisted hand.

A figure with a bleached skull as McNabb had never witnessed before, covering its face. A skull of protruding tusks and sharp bone.

Chapter 25

THE PERCUSSIVE SOUND of thunder had made both Malin and Kelley jump in shock, then laugh. Then they had continued walking. The two constantly moved around trees that looked to emerge and prevent any kind of path from forming. The sound of rain had come suddenly. They heard it battering at the leaves overhead and eventually, accepting they were not to find anything of interest in the darkness, they turned and made their way back.

Without the trees to cover them, they raced to the welcoming lights of the cottage, arriving dripping-wet yet in a joyous mood.

McNabb was back at his place at the kitchen table, shirtless and with a towel draped over his shoulders. Malin and Kelley both assumed the sweat, beaded and running down his body and hair was rainwater. His hands, almost black for the soil covering them, were wrapped around a fresh cup of tea. The sight of him quickly evaporated the playful mood from Malin and Kelley.

Malin, in fact, looked to him and felt as if he were seeing him for the very first time; a man he was yet to be introduced to.

Kelley cleared her throat and asked, "Anything?"

For a moment it was as if he had not heard her. Then he looked at her from beneath his eyebrows and took another moment to verbally respond.

The whites of his eyes, Malin observed, had

reddened.

"Nothing," McNabb answered. "I doubt there was anything to find, anyway."

"It was the flash of a camera," Malin insisted.

"Or the light of a low-flying plane," McNabb smirked.

"That's even worse than your first excuse," Malin snapped back.

"Excuse?" McNabb smirked all the more, shook his head as if in disbelief and brought his drink towards his lips. "There is no excuse… I thought I was expected to work with adults, not children struggling with their imagination."

"I think we're all tired," Kelley interjected before Malin could respond, "and the weather and sense of isolation combined are playing on that."

McNabb downed the contents of his cup and pulled the towel from his shoulders, permitting Malin to see he had a tattoo of a symbol of some kind on one of them. He dabbed his face with the towel, then patted his hair before dropping it onto the table as he got to his feet. He took a breath and released it as he smiled to them once again.

"I know rat traps have been placed around the cottage, but we're bound to still hear a couple of them scratching from within the walls and beneath the floors," he said. "Remember that, before you come running to my room, wanting me to hold your hands."

Chapter 26

THE DOOR TO his father's study was open, but only just. He caught sight of his parent, sitting in his office chair, holding a mobile phone to his ear that appeared so dated now yet was so advanced at the time.

"I'm being deadly serious," Sidney said down the line, "Marcus is going to have to–"

He swivelled around in his chair and momentarily looked to his son with wide eyes, as if he had been caught doing something questionable.

His eyes changed soon enough as he smiled, placed a hand over the mobile to keep what he was to next say between him and his son.

"Go get some ice cream from your mother," he quietly suggested, "and I'll be down in a minute."

Still smiling, he leaned forward, just enough to touch the door with his fingertips and pushed it shut.

And Sidney was no longer in his study. He was walking in tall grass, keeping close to the side of a building, with a Polaroid camera held at his side.

Not just any building, but Hewitson Cottage.

He stopped at the kitchen window, wiped dirt from a windowpane using his sleeve and peered inside as best he could. He waited a moment before lifting the camera. Pointing it into the kitchen, he pressed the button and there was a flash of light before he was outside no more.

He was in one of the front rooms of Hewitson Cottage. The same room, as fate would have it, that his son would come to stay in.

He stood at the window, but he did not look out. He did not look to his feet, but to one in particular. He looked at the foot he used to press down against a creaking floorboard.

Malin woke. It was dark in his room, but his eyes adjusted in good time. Looking up at the ceiling, he listened to the sound of the rain against the window and of the winds running alongside the outside walls. He wondered why he had dreamed of his father, and of why he had dreamed of him being *here*. His father, he was certain, would never have even heard of Hewitson Cottage.

Malin finally noticed the chill in the air and, pulling his sleeping bag tighter, rolled onto his side. It was then he noticed a dim light spilling onto the outside hallway. A faint, yellow light far too dim to be the moon or an electric light. He stared at it for a moment, trying to explain it as an item McNabb or Kelley may have brought with them. Freeing himself from his sleeping bag, he rose on unsteady legs and ventured to the door. The light coming from the window above the front door was just enough for him to see the door to McNabb's room was open. Curious, he turned his head and looked towards the kitchen.

He could see the table had been moved and the trapdoor had been propped open. The light he had become aware of was coming from the cellar.

Could he still be dreaming? Strangely, he felt as if he could still be asleep, that he was still in a dream. But a part of him knew that was not true; that he was standing at the doorway of his room, and a spectral light was coming from the cellar.

Malin looked to his wristwatch. The hands were meant to glow in the dark, but not enough for him to accurately tell the time. He swallowed, stepped out onto the landing, and crept towards the kitchen, becoming aware of the sound as he did so. It sounded as if someone were scraping, scratching. Rats, perhaps?

No, it was the sound of a shovel digging dirt, and rats wouldn't explain the light.

Malin felt the cold kitchen floor through his socks as he made his way to the trapdoor. He could see the wooden steps leading down onto a dirt floor. Standing over them, the digging sound had increased in volume.

The shadow of a man moved briefly across the cellar floor and Malin felt his body stiffen with panic, but no one appeared.

And then, the digging sound started all over again.

A treasure hunter of some kind?

No, the door to McNabb's room had been open, he remembered that now. Still anxious but confident it was most likely the university lecturer working beneath him, Malin took his first steps into the underground, leaning close against the wall as if it were to prevent him from falling if one of the old steps were to break beneath his weight. He crouched, knowing that doing so would reveal what awaited him a little sooner, and was relieved to see that he had been right; that McNabb was down there.

Relieved, but disturbed at what he was slowly forced to accept that he was seeing.

McNabb was digging a hole in the dirt floor, from

which the light appeared to be coming. At first, Malin wondered if a portable light of some kind was responsible but, once he truly saw the cellar, he could only look in horror.

The walls were covered in tiles, creating a grim mosaic depicting the miners that had been buried alive so long ago and Malin could have sworn the flickering shadows thrown by the uncanny light caused the men to appear as if they were moving, desperately trying to claw their way free.

"Who would want it to look like this?" he asked as he stepped away from the stairs. Only then did McNabb stop digging and, holding the shovel beside him, take a single step back.

Malin had a moment to notice the man's shadow, and how that unnatural light disturbed it so… McNabb's shadow was that of a bipedal, horned beast in possession of a scythe.

"Rupert," he asked softly, "what are you doing down here?"

Something took a tight hold of his foot. He jumped back in horror and looked down to see a skeletal hand had broken through the ground and briefly taken a hold of him. Now, its fingers desperately danced around the dirt in search of him.

"Jesus!"

He looked to where McNabb had been standing, desperate for any form of explanation, and found the spot empty. He was alone down here.

The ground beneath him began to shake as dust fell from above. The whole structure was moaning, walls ready to fall, and the filthy hands of the dead were emerging, one after the other in search of him.

The trapdoor slammed shut above him, but he couldn't bring himself to look back. The men of tile against the walls were all shifting now, looking to him with pleading eyes. He could *hear* their desperate moans and cries for help.

Hands without flesh scratched at his legs, trying to take hold, longing to pull him down to them.

Then a light so blinding, he instinctively brought a hand over his face to cover his eyes.

"Ryan–"

Kelley's voice. He blinked rapidly to try to bring his eyes to see what was before them.

"–is everything okay?"

A sixty-watt bulb hummed from the ceiling. Malin saw the basement for how it truly was. The modern water pump against the far wall, a water heater nearby.

Walls of lime green tiles and not some corrupt mosaic. Even the floor beneath him was solid concrete. Dusty, yes, with signs that work on a walk-in shower had been abandoned some time ago.

Malin turned in a circle, open mouthed, as he tried to make sense of what he had seen. There was no sign of McNabb; only beautiful Kelley, in her striped pyjamas and blue cotton bathrobe, looking at him with concern.

"Ryan," she started.

"I think I scared myself," he responded desperately, forcing an artificial smile. "Sleepwalking."

"Can you remember what frightened you? I heard you screaming."

He laughed, though it was one entirely of shame.

"Just a nightmare," he responded, heading towards the stairs, "I'm sorry for disturbing you, it was really nothing."

He felt her eyes on him until he had fully emerged from the basement. He could no longer hear rain and there was enough moonlight shining through the kitchen windows for him to see his way back to his room without difficulty.

He noticed McNabb's door was open, but only just.

PART 3

Chapter 27

MALIN WOKE, AND this time he was certain he would not return to sleep. He recalled a night of terrifying dreams. Dreams he could not recall on waking. But the dread remained.

And he recalled being in the basement, and what had seemingly occurred.

He sat, rubbed sleep from his eyes and looked to the windows. A pale grey sky, condensation upon the glass. He glanced at his watch and saw it was already past eight. He was hungry and he was cold, and he needed to empty his bladder... and the thought of using *that* toilet was worse than his cold and hunger combined.

Still, it was Saturday. Were they planning on leaving tomorrow, or waiting until Monday? He would have to ask. He assured himself that he had a good few thousand words to write about the place, but nowhere near enough for a full book about it – not yet. Currently, he would have to include plenty of the history he had uncovered over the years.

But all of these things could wait until later.

He rose and dressed hurriedly. The floorboard near the window groaned despite his being far from it. Malin froze, staring at it for a moment, before putting it down to the unstable temperature within the cottage. Stepping out into the hallway, he immediately noticed McNabb's bedroom door was fully open. He turned towards the kitchen, saw Kelley's door was fully closed, and found McNabb sitting at the table, his left hand buried within a cooler box. The lecturer, sitting with an irritated expression, raised his eyes to Malin and sneered.

"Eczema," he complained. "It must be all the dust in the air, or the damp. Take your pick."

"I'm sorry to hear that," Malin said as he made his way to the back door.

"Why? It's not as if you're responsible for it."

Malin chose not to respond and ventured onward.

Outside, the rain was a steady drizzle but as it fell on the leaves in the trees it sounded as if a heavy rain were falling. The bright plastic exterior of the porta-loo looked out of place, unnatural and perhaps nightmarish in its current surroundings. He knocked at the door, just to be certain Kelley was not in there, before pulling it open and stepping inside. The fresh air was replaced by a strong chemical smell. Malin urinated, flushed and returned to the cottage. Kelley was now in the kitchen, preparing some toast as she waited for the kettle to boil, still in her striped pyjamas and cotton gown. She smiled to Malin, though he saw quite clearly in her eyes how she was still concerned about the events some hours gone.

"Good morning," she said, "I'm having toast and coffee, if you'd like some?"

"Please," he smiled feebly as he pulled a chair from under the kitchen table, part expecting McNabb to voice a complaint of some kind.

"I was thinking," Kelley suggested, "we could find the entrance to the old mine today."

"The mine?" McNabb scoffed at the idea. "All you'll

find there would be broken bottles of Buckfast and dogged cigarette ends! The mine," he concluded, "I can't think of a bigger waste of time!"

Malin was surprised by his response and saw how Kelley was just as taken aback, if not more so.

"I'm sorry," Kelley responded, almost chuckling given her surprise, "but the mine is a vital part of Hewitson Cottage and its history."

"Then go and explore the abandoned mine," McNabb said as he turned to Malin and grinned. "I'm sure you and I could find something more interesting to look into, don't you think?"

"With all respect," Kelley interjected, "I assumed we were to stick together?"

McNabb sighed, shook his head at it all and removed his hand from the chiller box, permitting Malin an opportunity to observe how the skin was covered by red, painful-looking blotches. "Respect." he smirked, shaking water from his hand, "Of course… I'm only the most experienced member of our little expedition; but no, you do what you think is best. Just be considerate enough to let me know when the two of you return from your little trip."

"Rupert," she implored, but it was of no use; he had already departed the kitchen and was returning to his room.

"Is he okay?" Malin quietly asked.

"He must be tired," she replied in McNabb's defence a moment before fresh toast popped up from the toaster.

"Or sore," Malin suggested. "His hand looks bad."

"Yes," Kelley agreed, turning her back to him so she

could spread butter across the hot surface of the toast. "I've never known him to have such a flare-up."

Chapter 28

WHAT HAD STARTED as a light and consistent drizzle had become a torrential downpour. Malin was cold and uncomfortable. His shoes had long given up and allowed the water in, just as his face was dripping wet despite having his hood up. He knew they had been retracing their steps, heading back and forth in search of the entrance to the old mine. Given the choice, he might have surrendered a long time ago and begun the long walk back to the cottage.

And yet he was comfortable. Out here, the elements were undoubtedly challenging, yet he was glad to be there, with only Kelley for company.

"It's definitely around here somewhere," she insisted, turning back and stepping into her own footprints.

The dirt path they had been following was spacious enough, but the two could still see nothing more than trees. There had been a post some way back, old and decaying, the word MINE long carved into it with an arrow directing straight ahead, but Malin knew they could have since unintentionally ventured onto another, clearer path. The land had been left unattended for so long, he doubted even a map would have been much use.

"It *has* to be around here," Kelley said, ducking down low and venturing beneath the thick branches of nearby trees.

Malin considered the treacherous detour she was taking; at how quickly the rainwater was rushing along the ground, as if it were a stream. He re-examined her previous choice of words. How she could *feel* the mine was nearby. Had scientific study and explanation been cast aside, and so soon?

He reminded himself of how he had always been the pessimist. The weather, he decided, was why he was ready to head back.

He decided he would see this through, until both of them could say there was nothing more to say or do. Now crouching down to follow her. Nettles brushed against his hands almost immediately. He made a brief mental note to keep an eye open for dock leaves, then recalled how their use had always been a placebo effect. They would no longer work now he knew this.

Where was Kelley? How could she have travelled out of sight, and so quickly? Struggling to maintain his balance, he found himself tempted to call out for her. In fact, he had been just about to, right before he came out into a clearing.

The rain had caused the rockface before them to appear as raw gingerbread. The sight was so unexpected, it claimed Malin's breath. He couldn't believe it. He and Kelley were standing in a small semi-circle; a line of trees curving around them, the mountain immediately before them. Smiling, he turned and looked to Kelley and saw how she was staring upward. He followed her gaze. Trees were soon running along the rocky ground, bodies bending at unnatural angles. He realised the water coming down on them was pouring from the leaves and branches combined. Kelley lowered her chin, so she could look directly at Malin, and pointed to one side, to what looked to be the mouth of a cave.

"That must be the entrance to the old mine," she insisted and before he could voice his response, she had taken the flashlight from her pocket and was heading towards it.

"Let's not get our hopes up," Malin said, "it could just be any old cave."

But Kelley had been right. The tunnel sloped downward before coming to an abrupt and artificial end after a matter of metres. Long rusted sheets of corrugated iron had been erected to keep the curious from venturing any farther; a notice screwed into the centre of these warned of an unstable and deadly structure and a threat of trespassers being prosecuted.

Malin was certain he had noticed it first; how one of the lower sheets of iron had been pushed or pulled outward from their side, and how filthy, bare footprints led towards them. Someone had been on the other side of the barrier. Someone had ventured out from the darkness.

"Do you see that?" Kelley asked as she shone the beam of her torch over the footprints, following them back to where they first emerged.

"Probably a man, given the size," Malin said with a nod. "Could be someone living *off the grid…*"

"Or it could be *something* has come out."

Malin smiled, wondering if she were joking or seeing if his opinions could be so easily swayed. "They're a man's footprints," he insisted. "A man I'm pretty sure I'd rather avoid if I'm being completely honest."

"Haven't you ever been told to beware beasts coming as men?" she asked him, but before he could answer, she was moving onward.

"What are you doing?"

"There's a way in," she answered, kneeling before the opening. "Don't you want to see what's down there?"

"No," he laughed nervously, but she wasn't listening to him. She was already pushing herself through the narrow gap.

Chapter 29

THE AIR WAS bitterly cold, and as still as the resting dead.

A short distance beyond the barrier, a steep staircase of stone plunged into the depths. Kelley led the way, her torchlight shining over the wet stone. Malin could hear every movement they made and every breath that he took.

Whatever the light did not fall upon may as well have not been there. Everything else was impenetrable darkness.

They reached the final step. Kelley slipped, gasped, then giggled at her own feeling of surprise. Malin had reached forward and taken a firm hold of her elbow, fearing she would fall and be lost to the darkness. With his heartbeat pounding, he was reluctant to let her go.

He followed her along a passageway so narrow, his arms occasionally scraped along the sides.

"Thirty men died down here," Kelley said. "It took three weeks to retrieve the bodies."

"I believe so," Malin spoke quietly. For a moment he thought a moth had strayed into the light and he shuddered involuntarily.

"They only closed the mine because it was privately owned and Hewitson didn't want anything to do with the place," Kelley said. "He didn't even want to sell it, it's like he wanted to forget all about it."

Malin briefly thought of the man serving in Europe.

Had the trenches he had occupied been as narrow as this, and the nights just as dark?

What was Kelley hoping to achieve down here? It was madness!

"How are you feeling?" Kelley asked.

"Uncomfortable," he answered her with honesty.

"In what way?"

"It's crowded and we can't see a thing in front of us."

"We'll turn back, soon," she responded after a pause. "I'm wondering how anyone could possibly be staying down here."

"No one would come this far down," he reasoned. "The footprints were bare, remember? I can't see someone having no shoes but a decent torch."

"Maybe their eyes work better in the dark?"

Malin smirked. "I can't help but feel you're poking fun at me."

"Not at all," she claimed, "I'm genuinely interested in what you're thinking. What your thoughts about this place are."

"I'm thinking it's a broken ankle, waiting to happen."

"Did you know some mines used to invite wealthy locals down? They would even have musicians playing. Visitors could buy a candle and wander around, seeing how it was for the other half."

"You can't buy sense."

Kelley stopped so suddenly, Malin walked right into her. "What is it?" he asked.

"Nothing," she said. "I really don't think there is *anything* down here."

"I could have told you that," he laughed, though he was feeling somewhat annoyed.

"Are you ready to turn back, start the walk back to the cottage?"

He laughed again. "I didn't want to come down here to begin with."

"Where's your sense of adventure?" she asked, he could feel her smile through the darkness.

"I must have left it behind."

"Well, make sure you bring it next time," she joked. "But let's go. If we're lucky, the rain will have stopped."

But the rain had not stopped. It had worsened; the two excitedly spoke of their discovery during the long walk to the cottage as the skies grew darker and made promises of yet more thunder. Of course, the two discussed many a thing during the journey, but the topic continuously returned to the mine and the footprints before the barrier. Malin continued to insist they were those of an unfortunate, yet Kelley would ask, once more, if that was his *feeling*.

Malin did not want to discuss what he was feeling, not with her, for fear his confession would have her never speak to him again.

The first roll of thunder crawled across the skies as they reached the cottage, the one light coming from the kitchen. The two entered in high spirits but turned silent seeing McNabb, standing before the kitchen sink with his left arm plunged beyond the wrist in ice water and frozen bags of food.

"No better?" Kelley inquired, realising for the first time just how wet she was.

"No," McNabb answered, shaking his head. "You look soaked-through," he said to Malin. "Go dry off, get a change of clothes, and we'll examine the cellar. I have an experiment in mind."

It was clear to Malin that McNabb simply wanted him out of the room, to discuss something privately with Kelley, but granting him such opportunity did not sit right. He looked to Kelley however and seeing she didn't seem to be showing any sign of protest, he nodded in agreement.

"It'll be nice, changing back into dry clothes," he smiled weakly, hoping they would believe he was ignorant to what was occurring. "I'll be a couple of minutes," he concluded walking out of the room, granting the two their privacy.

"Well," McNabb asked Kelley in a desperate whisper, "what did he say?"

"Who?"

"Marcus," he said. "He called me, trying to get a hold of you!"

"Marcus? He hasn't," she started but stopped, looking to her mobile phone and seeing that the battery had given up without her realising. "For the love of– Phone's died," she sighed, holding it up for McNabb to see.

"Mine's on the table, take it and call him back, quickly," he insisted, "while you have the time to speak with him!"

The urgency in his voice was enough for her to quickly move forward and take his mobile phone from the table. "What is it? What's going on?"

"It's Malin's father," he said. "Marcus only knows what happened to him!"

Chapter 30

KELLEY IMMEDIATELY TOOK to scrolling down the list of contacts.

"Don't call him in here," McNabb advised, "not when Ryan could come walking in. Take it outside and I'll tell him you're using the toilet."

"That's a good idea," Kelley agreed, and she rushed back out into the rain, pulling her coat over her head with the hand she then used to pull the door of the porta-loo open. She hurried inside, locking the door behind her before sitting down on the lowered toilet seat. Drops of water on the screen of the mobile phone prevented her from calling, so she wiped the screen dry against her trouser leg and tried again. This time, the call went through. He answered on the second ring.

"Marcus," she said, "it's Kelley."

"I know who it is," he replied, sounding far from excited. "What's up?"

"You've been trying to call me!"

"Call you? No," Marcus informed her, "I'm pretty sure I haven't."

"Rupert told me you had been trying to reach me, he said you had information on Sidney Malin."

There was a moment of silence. Kelley began to wonder if the line had been disconnected and was about to ask if Marcus was still there on the line before he spoke once again.

"Kelley," he said, "I haven't spoken to either one of

you. I have no idea what you are talking about."

Fear clutched at her heart. She tried to resist it, tried to hope that this was all part of a silly misunderstanding.

"You must have," she insisted, back on her feet and unlocking the toilet door. "I just got back from the mine, and–" she fell silent, pushing the door open.

"What is it?" Marcus asked. "Kelley, what's going on?"

"It's Hewitson Cottage," she answered quietly. "It's disappeared."

"What do you mean," Marcus asked, "*It's disappeared*?"

"It isn't there," she said as she slowly moved forward, the falling rain no longer of any importance. "Hewitson Cottage has gone."

Chapter 31

Rupert McNabb – no, not McNabb, but the entity that had claimed him – withdrew his hand from the frozen water. The bones of the hand were curled and stiff. Some of the flesh had fallen away, some of it was rotting.

This body would not last much longer.

Of course, it hadn't been intended to last too long.

It wasn't a case of just any body being suitable. McNabb's, for example, would most likely fall beyond repair before he reached the gate of the property.

A strong mind was needed, a brain that operated on certain levels, or was at least capable of doing so.

In the front bedroom of Hewitson Cottage, Malin stood with a towel around his shoulders and concluded drying his hair with another. Looking to the window, he couldn't explain the arrival of the dense fog he saw outside. It almost solidified as it touched the glass and permitted nothing to be seen beyond it.

A cold, damp hand pressed against his shoulder. Startled, he turned to look back and found himself entirely alone. The floorboard near the window creaked.

Kelley pushed slowly through the tall grass. Left hand in the air, she moved her fingers in delicate patterns. The effect it had was like watching a child playing with sparklers.

"It's still here," she informed Marcus, "it's just not in this time."

"What does that mean? Can you get to him?"

"I think so," she said, "but it's going to take a lot of concentration."

"Call me when it's done."

Chapter 32

MALIN CLOSED HIS eyes and took a deep breath.

He needed to calm himself, that was all. He was tired and uncomfortable; the long walk in the rain would do that. Then there was the brief exploration of the mine.

Eyes still closed, he thought of the many places he had worked before here. Granted, he had company on this trip, but they were secluded from everything and anything else.

Exhaustion, he told himself, *and seclusion.*

He released another breath, opened his eyes and couldn't quite believe what he saw. The mist on the other side of the window looked to have settled into an entirely solid form.

But he smiled.

He smiled because, although he had never experienced anything like this, he knew he would most likely find an explanation within a heartbeat were he to look online. It would all be caused by a trick of the light, or the lack of it.

The door to his room slammed shut. Malin turned on his heels, heart pounding at the sudden and violent noise. He looked at it for a second or so, then walked towards it.

"Kelley? Rupert?"

Why was his heart still pounding? The back door of the cottage had been wide open, a gust of wind could have easily been responsible.

He took the door handle, turned it and pulled the door open. Looking out onto the corridor, everything appeared as it seemed, and he cursed his sense of unease because of it. He knew he could step out of the room and be at once capable of seeing McNabb in his place at the kitchen. He stepped out of the hallway–

–and found himself back in the room, standing before the closed door.

He gasped in alarm and staggered back. How could this be? Was he hallucinating? Could this be related to the mass hysteria that Kelley had wanted to discuss in her essay?

Could McNabb have hypnotised him, or had his time in the mine exposed him to some form of hallucinogenic fungus?

"Stop panicking," he hissed under his breath.

Malin moved forward again and regained as much of his composure as he could before taking hold of the door handle for a second time.

"Don't be paranoid and don't be scared," he told himself, "just leave your eyes and your mind open."

He pulled the door open. The appearance of the hallway had changed; everything looked to have been touched by a delicate grey light.

Everything was utterly silent.

No, not everything… he could hear the ticking of a clock, coming from the kitchen.

Malin took another breath and stepped out of the room, only to find himself staring at that same, closed door.

"No!" he screamed and fell to his knees, hands holding at his head. "What's happening?" he cried.

"Ryan," a soothing voice said from his back, "you have to listen to me, because what I'm about to say is so important."

Tears were already at his eyes.

"No," he croaked, "not this…"

"Ryan," the voice pleaded, "you *have* to listen to me."

He wept openly, wiped the tears from his eyes against his wrist and looked back.

Jemma was standing there.

Lightning carved the sky.

As heavy rain fell, Kelley remained standing. The rain poured down her face, into her eyes, almost blinding her, but she did not attempt to wipe it away, not for an instant.

With hands held out, her fingers continued to move, leaving what looked like red-hot lines that remained in the air for a second. In her mind, she repeated words that man had forgotten hundreds of years earlier.

A shape began to appear in the vacant space where she knew Hewitson Cottage should be standing. So delicate at first, it would have easily been dismissed as mist or an artifact of the light through the pouring rain.

Kelley held onto what she had seen and continued. Her reward was as the glimpse began to materialise and become a structure. Hewitson Cottage had reappeared. She could stop.

She allowed herself to smile at her achievement, then smiled all the more on seeing the corrugated iron covering the doors and windows of the property.

"Please," she said, "don't you see me as *any* kind of

challenge?"

It took the subtlest of movements from her fingers to have the board upon the door crumple forward as if it were paper, then it was completely removed and tossed to one side. She moved her hand as if she were brushing aside a curtain and what looked like hundreds of fireflies emerged from the air in front of her and slowly drifted towards the open door, illuminating her path.

Kelley finally pulled her coat tight to keep the rain from her and took confident strides to the open door of Hewitson Cottage.

Chapter 33

JEMMA LOOKED AS beautiful in death as she had in life, but her appearance did nothing to calm Malin.

"Am I dead?" he cried. "Mad?"

"You should never have doubted your sanity," she assured him, "not for an instant. You've no idea how right you are, and how close you have come to making contact. I've wanted – *needed* – to speak with you for so long."

"Well," he sobbed, "why now? Answer me," he pleaded, "am I dead?"

"You're alive," Jemma said, "and it's easier for me to speak with you, between times, but you have it within you to speak to so many others. You just have to believe *her* one final time, and you will be safely away from here. When you're safe," she pleaded, "you have to remember this: Ian isn't with me, a spirit claimed him and won't let him rest.

"You have to help him."

"Help him? How? Tell me what to do!"

Marie seemed to appear, looking out from behind her mother's legs. Malin saw her, saw the worry on her face, and hated himself for being in such a state before her.

"Marie," he smiled, and then he chuckled, "is that *really* you?" he asked as he scurried towards her on all fours. The child went to move away but was kept in place by her mother putting a hand against the back of her head. Malin noticed it. He saw how he had scared her, he simply refused to admit it, even to himself.

"I hope you're happy," he said and, with tears streaming down his face, he pressed the palm of his hand against her cheek. What felt like a mild, electrical current, ran over his skin.

"I hope you're happy," he repeated.

She did not respond. The change upon her was almost instantaneous; she froze and became as marble. Malin pulled away in horror and looked to her mother for an explanation.

"Jemma," he began, but it was already too late. She too had become white marble, mother and daughter appearing as ancient statues.

The crack was a hairline fracture, to begin with – a delicate blemish upon the cheek of the child, where Malin had so recently placed his hand. But it spread and it widened as it did so, and the firm white stone rapidly became crumbling grey, the cracks consuming mother and daughter both until they collapsed into rubble before him. Malin took handfuls of the stone, a part of him believing he could somehow put them back together, but every piece crumbled to dust within his hands and seeped out between his fingers.

Kelley entered the cottage; the majority of the guiding lights she had brought into creation turned into the room claimed by Malin, while the others continued to move throughout the building. She stepped into the front room to find him facing the window, his back to her.

"Ryan," she said as the burning lights circled him, "we have to leave. Ryan?"

She rushed around him and at once realised why he had neither responded nor budged. He stood in a trance, eyes rolled to the back of his head.

"Ryan," she asked calmly, "can you hear me?"

"You're here, thank God!" McNabb said, stumbling into the room. "There's something going on here."

Kelley stared at him, maintaining her silence. The only sound appeared to be that of McNabb's laboured breathing. He pushed his spectacles up along his nose and asked, "What is it? What are you thinking?"

"I'm thinking I can't blame you for trying," she smirked, "because you wouldn't know I now see you for what you are."

She gracefully moved two fingers upward and the knife that had been concealed at the back of McNabb's waistline was flung into the air with such force, the blade was imbedded in the ceiling. He looked up towards it, then lowered his head to smile at her. Holding his left hand to his side, it would have looked like he was pretending to be holding onto something. The shadow caused by the lights moving around the room, however, revealed a scythe in his possession, as well as tusks protruding from his face.

"The doctor was right about you," he grinned, "you are not to be underestimated…"

"You have his memories?"

"And Ryan's," he boasted, "and those of another."

"Then take a good look at what Rupert McNabb knows about me," she challenged, "before you try and do anything else."

"All I want is to survive, and to be free to leave this place. Would that really have you view me as such a monster?"

"Rupert's soul… Malin's… you'd damn them both, for your own gain?"

McNabb grinned. In the darkness, the blood covering his teeth appeared black.

"And how many of your own kind have you damned, and have you really convinced yourself that the damning of one is justified if it means another can be left in peace? This good doctor was right about you," he chuckled. "You're little more than a pretty attack dog on a tight leash."

"And you might have been powerful, once," she snapped, "but now you are old and weak. Stop this now and return to your slumber, or I will finish you here. Actually, no," she smiled, "I will leave you here with nothing. You'll be little more than a spirit, with no means of reaching out to any other soul, and unable to truly rest because of it."

"How dare you!" McNabb screamed and as he did so, decaying teeth fell from his gums and scattered across the floor. "When your ancestors first spilled blood over the dirt and begged for power, I was one of those that blessed them!"

"Times change," Kelley responded calmly, "things change, and the world has changed more than you can imagine. I'm offering you mercy," she said, "by giving you the opportunity to rest."

McNabb clutched at his chest, groaned in pain and stumbled back. Once against the wall, he slid down onto the ground. Kelley did not show the slightest sign of pity.

"Give me Malin," he pleaded. "Give him to me and

together, you and I shall walk away from this wretched ground, and I will show you true power."

"I'm sorry," Kelley said, "but there's nothing you could ever offer me that I'd really need."

"Well," he smirked, "I guess you'll just have to make him a better offer." And with that his eyes closed as his chin lowered slowly to his chest. Kelley took one last look at him, then turned her attention back on Malin. His eyes still looked entirely white.

"Ryan," she said clearly as she placed a hand against his face. "Ryan? Oh," she sighed, "if this is how we're going to have to do it…"

Kelley took his face in her hands and, closing her eyes, pressed her forehead against his own.

Chapter 34

HE TRIED – and failed – to recall what he had been doing a moment ago, just as he failed to recognise this place.

Malin's first assumption was that he was in a luxury hotel of some kind. He looked down, to the thick cream carpet he was standing on, turned and looked back to the leather couch and armchair facing the huge TV up on the wall.

Two doors beside one another on the wall immediately ahead, another door to the wall at his side. The door to his side, he reasoned, must lead out onto the hotel landing.

But there was more to the room he was in than the TV and furniture. There was a tall, oak unit with shelves crammed with books and DVDs and CDs. It didn't seem right, not for a hotel room.

"Are you still here?" Amy asked him as she walked out of one of the doors in front of him. She was fastening the green bathrobe he had been convinced she would never replace and, although her hair was a little messy and she was without makeup, she maintained her natural beauty. She always had done.

He thought he was about to lose consciousness.

"I thought you would have already been at the library," she said, and she stopped to peck him on the cheek before continuing to the other side of the room, turning on the TV – BBC News.

He noticed the curtains and wondered how he

hadn't seen them earlier. Grey curtains, drawn. He considered walking right over to those curtains and taking a look at the world outside.

He heard the cat meow an instant before he felt its cheek rub against his leg. He looked down, saw a large black cat purring as it affectionately placed its own scent against his jeans. "We used to talk about getting one," he said, though he wasn't entirely certain he had opened his mouth to say it.

"And we did," Amy smiled. "Look at her," she said, looking at the cat, "she thinks you're her dear daddy."

The cat looked up to him with large, beautiful eyes and then it walked close enough to the shelving unit for it to leap atop the highest point and get comfortable. Malin recalled how cats felt most comfortable from up high, where they could survey all of their possessions.

The door beside previously used by Amy was pushed open and Kelley hurried into the room. Malin panicked. For a moment, he didn't have any idea to who she was.

"Kelley," he said, coming to his senses.

"Ryan, we have to hurry up and get out of here."

"No," Amy answered quickly, and she took his hand in her own. "You can't trust her and even a part of you must know that. You need to stay with me," she pleaded. "I want to give you everything you want, but she's only interested in taking what she needs."

"Ryan, I'm not even going to pretend *she* is here, but you have to listen to me and do as I say. I mean," Kelley said, hurrying over to the curtains, "just open your eyes and look at this!"

"Don't you open those curtains!" Amy yelled, but it

was too late. Kelley pulled one open with such force the rail came free of the wall and fell to the ground. Beyond the glass, Malin saw the room he had been staying in at Hewitson Cottage. He saw how the broken fragments of Jemma and Marie were still piled upon the floor.

He felt something catch at the back of his throat.

"Ryan," Kelley implored, walking to him, "we have to —"

He disappeared without a trace before she could say the next word. Amy turned and returned to the room she had come from, closing the door shut behind her.

"Son of a bitch!"

He heard the delicate singing of birds.

Malin took a breath as if he had just recalled his need to; then he took in his surroundings. He was back in the front room of Hewitson Cottage. He quickly looked down to the ground, expecting to see… what had he believed was there? He saw nothing out of the ordinary now, nothing whatsoever.

The floorboard near the window groaned. Malin turned to the sound and lost his breath.

His father was knelt near the window, carefully removing one of the floorboards from its place. He took the collection of cards from his side just as carefully.

No, not cards… they were photographs he had taken with a Polaroid camera. One by one, he dropped them into the opening he had made.

A photograph of the sealed entrance to the mine.

A photograph of Hewitson Cottage, taken from a

distance.

A photograph taken from outside the kitchen window, showing the spectral shape of three figures sat at a table.

A number of photographs taken within the kitchen, showing nothing at all out of the ordinary.

Sidney took a digital recorder from the windowsill and pressed his thumb down upon the record button. "There's definitely something here," he announced clearly, "and it has no intention of letting me leave without it. It's managed to disrupt the workings of my mobile," he laughed, "so I can't even guarantee you'll hear this. But if you do, we need a warlock here. I'll try keeping it distracted until you arrive here and hopefully find this, before it tricks me into destroying it."

He finished his recording and gently dropped the recorder into the embrace of the cool darkness. Sidney took a long breath, released it, and placed the floorboard back into its place, twice pressing down on it to secure it.

"It could be showing you this for two reasons," McNabb explained, confidently entering the room. "The first is with hopes of intimidating you. What choice could you possibly have if it bettered your father so easily?

"The second reason," he once more revealed his large, white teeth, grinning, "is to try and turn you against us. How can you trust us, when we kept so quiet about your missing father and were happy for you to believe he simply walked out on you and your mum?"

"Have you come to get me out of here?"

McNabb smiled, but it was one of sadness. "Kelley will get you out of here, I'm sure of it. I'm just here to say my goodbyes, and that it was a pleasure knowing you. And I'm sorry that I let you down… I just hope you learn from my mistake and don't believe it.

"It won't get you the love you want," McNabb warned him. "It might give you an impression of it, but it will be nothing more than a cheap and heartless replica of what you lost. Make the most of the true love you can get, and never take it for granted."

"Ryan!" Kelley cried out as she rushed into the room and, with her arrival, McNabb had simply vanished.

"Kelley," Malin said back at once, but she was gone just as suddenly as McNabb before her. The room had gone. There was nothing.

Chapter 35

AMY AFFECTIONATELY SQUEEZED his hand that little bit tighter and Malin found himself in the World Cinema section of HMV.

Found himself *back* in the World Cinema Section of the store, he thought. He didn't take in the writing or the images on the covers; he tried to remember what daydream he had just been pulled out of. Was there a haunted cottage? Had it been inspired by his latest bout of research, or a film he had watched many years ago?

"I can't believe we still don't own a copy of this," Amy laughed, taking a DVD from the display for them to examine. It was *Pan's Labyrinth* – the first movie the two had ever stayed in to watch together.

"Do you still think the last couple of minutes ruin it?" she laughed; and she looked him in the eyes, and he felt pure happiness. He wanted to bring her close and hold her. He wanted to brush his cheek against her own before resting his chin atop of her head.

Walk on the Wild side played across the store speakers. He remembered discussing the track with her in a small bar during the early hours and somehow felt even happier. Everything was perfect. Everything was as he would have wanted it.

When Kelley hurried out of the door that had been marked for staff use only, he didn't immediately recognise her, but he felt seeing her wasn't a good sign. Had he argued with her in a club one night? Had he–

"Ryan," she said, drawing closer, "we have to get going – now."

"I know," he responded instinctively, then wondered how he could betray himself in such a manner.

"Ryan," Amy said as she turned him around to face her, to look back into *those* eyes, "walk away from her and don't look back. You can't trust her."

"No," he smiled although his heart was breaking, "I can't trust myself… I know *you* aren't really you… But you know I'd do anything for this, and I know I have to go because of it, and now, before I happily accept this lie.

"Kelley," he said, turning away from Amy, hand slipping free from her own, "please take me away from here."

Kelley pulled her eyes open and took a breath as if she had been holding it underwater for too long. She parted her forehead from Malin's, registered the flickering of his eyes and tried to hold him up as he dropped to the ground.

She had prevented him from cracking his skull on the floorboards, but he was far heavier than she had been prepared for.

"Ryan," she hissed, "you're going to have to help me. I don't know if I can get you out – not on my own."

She glanced back over her shoulder and jumped at what she saw.

A kitchen chair had been dragged into the room for McNabb to pry the knife from the ceiling. Then she saw how he was still in the process of dragging himself towards her, knife in hand, body rapidly weakening.

She heard fingers break as he clawed his way closer.

"No," he pleaded, "you mustn't take him! Don't let him–"

"You've rested before," she growled, "this is the last chance I will give you to rest again."

Malin gasped as his eyes opened wide and he struggled to remember where he was. They darted over the ceiling before settling on Kelley. He took a tight hold of her shoulders and simply said her name. She didn't look at him. She maintained every ounce of her focus upon the ever approaching, broken figure.

"I won't let you take him, not without me." McNabb screeched as the hair fell from his scalp in clumps. "I won't be forced to remain here, forgotten!"

"Then burn," Kelley responded coldly, and she moved a hand so minutely, Malin didn't even see it. But he saw the flames that leaped at the edge of his vision, and he heard the scream of pain and defeat that surely belonged in a nightmare.

Despite the sight of a blackening corpse being consumed by fire, despite the sight of flames spreading and claiming his nearest possessions, Malin's pride managed to take a dent as he realised exactly how dependent he was on Kelley's support, simply to get into a sitting position.

"You can't rely on me, not here," she told him. "You're going to have to help me as best you–"

The spectre appeared, drawing out an animalistic howl. A figure standing tall in rotting furs that Malin could smell, its face covered by a grotesque skull, a scythe in its twisted hands. It looked down at Malin and although he couldn't see the eyes of the creature, he could feel them fix upon him.

Howling once more, it held its scythe high and brought it swinging down at Malin. He screamed, covered his head with his arms and immediately lost consciousness, experiencing a pain like he had never felt before.

PART 4

Chapter 36

He was cast back to the moment in which he set eyes on Amy Moers for the first time. How beautiful, *radiant* she looked as she walked by in her mustard cardigan. She may not have noticed him, but he knew his very soul had seen her.

And he saw Amy, smiling to him in her favourite Cansei de Ser Sexy t-shirt, and he swore to himself that he would never allow anyone to hurt her.

And then he saw her crying silently, and he knew that he was the only monster to blame.

It felt as if he were being shaken, as if someone were trying to awaken him. Malin at once felt it was Ian, trying to wake him so he would not miss the bus to college.

He longed to be woken, because then the torture of being forced to see all he had lost and the hurt he had caused could be taken from him.

He woke, realised it was the Ford Transit shuddering as it bounced along an uneven path that had brought him back to consciousness. Slumped across the passenger side, his forehead repeatedly bumping against the cold window, trees flashig past in the gloom. Malin pulled himself into a more stable position and looked to Kelley. He saw her hands, lit by the dashboard tight against the wheel, knuckles white, and the perspiration at her brow. Slowly, he placed a hand against his chest and slowly withdrew it to be examined.

"It was a psychic attack," Kelley explained the lack of blood for him. "You weren't physically harmed."

She was beautiful. Despite everything else that was occurring, perhaps *because* of everything else that was occurring, he truly saw her beauty. No, he didn't just see it, he felt it inside of him. Malin was in love with Kelley Stranack. He loved her in a way he never thought he would be able to again, not after losing Amy.

It was all enough to have him feel so at ease. Comforted. He smiled, leaned against the passenger window once more, offering his shoulder to take the bumps this time. He looked into the wingmirror. He saw Hewitson Cottage ablaze. The flames had taken the tall grass and were threatening to claim the lanky trees, hungrily advancing towards the painfully lumbering Transit van. But they had made it out of there, *together*. That was what really mattered, he was sure of that.

He was dazed, he was aware of that much. It was a drunk feeling. He managed a smile as he took to securing his seatbelt.

But where was the buckle?

It was too dark inside the van for him to see it. His hands felt where he thought it should be and found nothing. Confused, he took a breath and released it, looked to the windscreen as if for inspiration and saw the chained and padlocked gate they had come through days earlier.

It was coming closer and closer, and Kelley wasn't lowering their speed, wasn't talking about jumping out to unlock the gate. Feeling a growing sense of concern, Malin turned to say something, he just couldn't think of the words.

He didn't have to.

Kelley took her right hand from the wheel and held it with her palm facing the windscreen, her fingers and thumb stretched out. She brought the three fingers farthest from her thumb back to the palm and muttered something he didn't understand.

Suddenly, she appeared to be holding a crystal beneath those closed fingers. It went from gently glowing to a blaze that began to consume the inside of the vehicle – Malin could feel its warmth spreading all over, relaxing him.

And he looked to the windscreen and saw the chain and padlock shatter into countless pieces, right before they drove straight into the gate and the impact sent him towards the dashboard.

Malin opened his eyes and at once accepted that he was in hospital.

The dull tone of paint on the walls, the moisture stain on the ceiling, simply how old the other, unoccupied beds in the room appeared was enough for him to know that this was no private hospital. This was an NHS hospital, left to rot and ruin under Conservative rule. They wanted people like him to look at the state of disrepair and to claim that privatisation was the only way forward, but he would never do that for them. He would never be taken in.

"You're awake," a voice delicately announced to his left.

Malin almost jumped in alarm, realised his left eye

was in fact covered with surgical dressing.

His neck ached as he slowly turned to look to his left, searching for his unknown companion. He accepted the pain at his neck, along with that in his ribs and shoulder, were presently lessened with use of moderately strong painkillers.

"Please," the voice said, "it'll be easier for you if I move my chair…"

It was too late. Malin was looking to him now; Malin was trying to understand what 'look' the man was hoping to achieve, and he doubted the man knew for himself. The turtleneck sweater belonged on an art teacher somewhere, but the blazer and pressed trousers were those of a politician. The neatly trimmed goatee beard may, or may *not*, have explained the open-toe sandals, Malin just couldn't be sure. He wondered if he could be hallucinating as he failed to comprehend what this guest hoped to represent.

But there was more than that, and he was convinced of it. He was sure his visitor was even struggling to comprehend what he had hoped to represent.

Malin opened his mouth to ask if he existed and found himself struggling to talk, his mouth was so dry.

"Let me help you," the man insisted in a well-spoken, educated tone Malin felt was artificial, it seemed far too staged to be natural. He took a pitcher of water from the corner table and began to pour some into a Styrofoam cup. "Ryan," he said, "I'm going to do what is best here and simply tear the plaster from the graze on your knee – you are never going to see Kelley Stranack ever again."

Malin accepted the water because his throat felt as if it had been lined with sandpaper. He insisted on refusing any help and struggled to bring the cup to his mouth, drinking just enough to ease the thirst. Despite how little he consumed, his entire body seemed to suffer for his drinking.

"Who are you?" he croaked. "What is it you want?"

The man smiled and said, "My name is Marcus–"

Marcus! He recalled his father saying that name so many years ago, just as he recalled McNabb saying it so recently.

"–and not only am I here to answer any questions you may have, but to give you the advice you sorely need. With an excellent opportunity thrown in," he smiled, "of course."

Chapter 37

MALIN DEMANDED TO know where Kelley was, though he knew he was in no real position to demand anything. Too exhausted and sore to move from the hospital bed, he briefly considered hurling the water at Marcus but was forced to accept even that would be too strenuous a motion.

"Kelley brought you here in one piece," Marcus answered flatly, "and then she informed me of the most recent of events. I imagine she is writing up her report as we speak."

Malin recalled their confrontation with McNabb. He saw Hewitson Cottage ablaze in his mind and wearily asked, "Her university report?"

Marcus smiled. "Kelley was not… *is* not a university student. Kelley works for me. The university has received very generous payments from the organisation we are a part of over the years, so they were willing to briefly add her to the system. All traces of her will be removed by now, however."

"Your organisation? If she's not a student, what is she? Where is she?" he asked.

"Kelley identifies… as a sorceress," Marcus replied, and without a smile. "amongst other things. The organisation I speak of is worldwide and has kept all supernatural beings safe from the public for much longer than you can ever possibly imagine. But you must understand," he paused as he struggled to find the most suitable way to explain, "sometimes, to protect the majority of supernatural and paranormal beings, you simply have to take care of the worst of them."

"Are you expecting me to believe this? Is this all some... some... some Derren Brown stunt?"

Marcus laughed. "No," he grinned, "I know this may be difficult for you to accept but I'm sure you will. Your father was one of us."

"My dad worked in insurance."

"Yes," Marcus smirked, "something of a private joke between us. Did you know I sent him to investigate Hewitson Cottage when you were still a child? He disappeared. Once it appeared certain he would not be returning, I posted a letter, supposedly from him, to your mother, alongside a cheque, to see you both taken care of."

"Why are you saying this?"

"Because your father was phenomenally talented. Think of the FBI profiler in those popular television shows or movies; multiply their talent by a fantastic amount and imagine them investigating potential supernatural or paranormal threats." He smiled gently before concluding, "And you are close to approaching what he did and just how valuable he truly was."

"Where's Kelley? I need to talk to Kelley!"

Marcus sighed. "I believe it really is for the best that you don't."

"Why? What have you done with her?"

"I'm afraid you will be more upset about what she has done to you... do you remember the day you met her?" Marcus asked. "You ordered a drink at Organico, and the waitress in a Joy Division t-shirt served you and, soon after, you met Kelley for the first time?

"The girl who served you is Kelley's partner, and the disposable cup she handed to you was a representation of her feelings towards Kelley. A simple spell and when you saw Kelley, you immediately began to develop those same feelings for her. I'm afraid we simply couldn't risk you deciding not to come to Hewitson Cottage, and so I insisted on the deception and I apologise. If it means anything," he shrugged, "I'm sure you'll get over her soon enough.

"They say there is a thin line that separates genius from madness, and so I believe the line that separates love from hate must be ever finer. Focus on the hate," he advised, "focus on how you needed to be manipulated, and I'm sure you'll be over it even sooner."

"Why me?" Malin asked, and he had never before heard himself sounding so defeated, so pitiful. "Why am I so important?"

Marcus smiled to him, pityingly. And Malin hated him for it.

"I'm going to give you my personal number," Marcus said, taking a slim card from a silver case tucked inside the pocket of his blazer, "and I would like you to consider calling me. In fact," he smiled, "I would like you to consider your working alongside us. I believe you have the same gifts your father had. You simply haven't been shown how to use them."

He held the card out for Malin to take. He waited a moment, then slowly accepted it. The card advertised a store of some kind named Crystal Energy, the address and telephone number placed between a promise of having everything a practitioner of alternative beliefs would ever require.

"There's a good lad," Marcus said. He got to his feet and walked to the door. "I'm not being rude, but I really have other business to attend to. I'm sure," he smiled, "any questions you may have will soon be answered… It's just I won't be here to witness it."

Marcus winked knowingly and stepped out of sight, gently closing the door shut behind him. Malin sighed and looked to the card. He read the same words over and over again, as if they were expected to suddenly change. When he heard the door open again, he thought it would be Marcus.

But it wasn't, it was his father, and he hadn't aged a day in all the years since he had last seen him. Wearing a smart suit and carrying a tabloid newspaper under his arm, he looked as if his being here was the most natural thing that could have ever occurred.

"Look at you," he smiled, "you're all grown-up."

Chapter 38

SIDNEY TOOK OWNERSHIP of the chair previously claimed by Marcus and went to leafing through the pages of the newspaper as if he were simply looking for the TV section. "You're right about Marcus – the accent is a put-on," he grinned. "He thinks people will take him more seriously, if he gives them the whole privately educated routine."

"I don't understand," Malin croaked.

"Well, it's like he said. There *are* werewolves and witches and all manner of things, and for the majority of them, we assist them in having as safe and normal a life as possible. But there are some, a minority," he explained, "that we have to come down on. Think about it," he shrugged, "when a poodle bites a small child, you don't destroy all poodles, do you? Just the one that can't be tamed. Still, Marcus would rather we didn't have to do any of that."

"No," Malin said blinking a tear away, "I don't understand how you're here... How you haven't changed over the years..."

Sidney smiled. It was a smile of relief, or of pity, but certainly not both, and Malin couldn't be sure which.

"A lot more happened at Hewitson Cottage than is publicly known of." he said. "I was sent to investigate. During my investigation, I learned Hewiton's miners had disturbed an ancient, pre-Christian power. It didn't simply long to be worshipped anymore. It's age and abandonment had quite possibly driven it mad."

"I could sense that," Malin breathed, "the desperation."

Sidney nodded, "Fortunately, it couldn't travel too far from its own sacred ground. It could only trouble those it had forged some kind of bond with, or those unfortunate enough to cross its path." He laid the newspaper in his lap and leaned forward.

"It recognised me as a threat, due to my rare gifts, and wanted to claim my body as a vessel, enabling it to travel. Of course, when I had proven myself to be no pushover, it kept me prisoner in a reality of its own making. It hoped I would eventually surrender my will to it to break the stalemate we were locked in. Clearly," he boasted, "I didn't.

"But I began to fear it may eventually claim a victory. Many a time it almost convinced me that I had escaped when, really, I hadn't. It merely wanted me to wander on with it on my back, growing in strength." His eyes met with Malin's, with the son who's life had passed him by.

"And then I began to wonder how old you were. Where I was kept, there was no sense of time as we understand it. I may have been held captive for one hour, I may have been there long after my human remains had turned to dust, but I had to take the chance and so I reached out and felt your mind, having always believed you possessed the same gifts as I and your great grandfather before you.

"After that," he shrugged, "it was relatively easy getting a few messages to Marcus and his merry band. Given the situation I was in, I couldn't exactly let them know that it was me reaching out, but I made it obvious that something at Hewitson Cottage was requesting *you* specifically. Having managed to keep the area quiet for so long, given my endless tussle with the old deity I knew an investigation would immediately be underway.

"The thing that troubled Hewitson Cottage and the surrounding area knew that people were coming. I managed to keep the most important parts from it, despite how difficult that proved. It sensed your gifts and wanted to wear you down until, defeated, you would have no option but to let it claim you and permit it to walk the land freely."

"Then why did it claim Rupert?"

"McNabb was a great man, once. An expert in his field, churning out ridiculous theories and giving lectures at such unbelievable events, all to keep people from knowing what was really out there. Unfortunately, as he got older," he sighed, "the man's heart simply desired more. No matter how much he denied this to himself. The threat he had come to investigate could easily take advantage of this.

"I believe it claimed McNabb at the first opportunity, simply to approach you at an unexpected angle. It may have literally wanted to use his physical form to inflict damage on you, while it also targeted your mind and beliefs. Fortunately," he smiled, "you had the witch – forgive me, *sorceress* – to assist you. With my unseen help, the two of you managed to overcome a powerful, yet out of practice entity."

Malin nodded and simply muttered, "Kelley."

"It might seem a bit of a cruel trick," Sidney said, "having you fall for her, but you simply have to get over it," he laughed. "You're probably barking up the wrong tree with her anyway. And as for our enemy, it couldn't take a look at what I knew without revealing a little knowledge of its own. It as good as handed me the manual on how to put it to sleep, once and for all, while it was preoccupied with the fire and your escape."

Malin stared across the room for a few moments in silence. So much to take in. He looked back to his long-lost father, "What are you going to do now… about Mum?"

Sidney took a deep breath and released it. "Officially, I'm not here. I'm still missing," he said. "Probably best for your mother to believe I'm dead, or whatever she had come to accept. She can continue with her life, and I will see what I can do with mine. But I'm sure you and I will bump into one another, from time to time, if you accept any of what Marcus has had to offer you."

"I can't believe you're saying this! I can't believe you could be so emotionless!"

"No, not emotionless," Sidney sighed, getting to his feet, "simply *wise*. Maybe you want to tell everybody what happened. Maybe you want to write it all down for your publisher? No one will believe you, and no one will ever risk printing your words, believe me.

"You can either choose to turn away from what you know, or you can embrace it. The choice is one you have to make on your own."

Sidney dropped the newspaper onto Malin's lap and walked out of the room without another word. His son struggled to digest all that had happened and so it took him a moment to realise why he had been given the newspaper, folded to reveal small article. It claimed Rupert McNabb, whilst researching his latest book, had perished in a terrible fire.

Malin signed himself out of hospital that same evening.

Chapter 39

IT STARTED WITH *You're Gonna Come Around* by Matt Barton with Dave Owen and The Carers. Soon, his heartbreak and his melancholy had an entire soundtrack. *Here Today, Gone Tomorrow* by The Ramones was followed by Blur's *You're So Great*; in honour of when he first saw her. He soon added Taylor Swift's *Seven* and followed this with Zuzu's *The Van Is Evil* on hearing it and immediately recalling their last journey together.

Malin had tried calling Kelley, only to learn her number was not recognised. Emails to her were bounced back. She no longer had any form of online presence.

The nights were the worst. One dream after another of her; in some he displayed grand gestures, in others the two merely completed the most mundane of tasks such as shopping. But regardless of what he dreamt, he woke immediately after, feeling utterly beaten.

He told himself that it wasn't real, that none of his feelings had been real, and that his last chance of truly being happy had been with Amy.

His apartment contained reminders of Amy he had simply overlooked but now seemed impossible to ignore. His apartment had become as a mausoleum to lost love.

He looked to his laptop. Writing seemed a waste of energy now. Practically every volume of *Malin's Mysteries* had, of course, been dedicated to Amy. He smiled in defeat. Dedicating another book to her would be akin to dedicating it to a ghost.

But did it really have to be that way?

It struck him as if from nowhere. For the first time in so long, he felt it.

Hope.

He was going to be happy with Amy, as he always should have been.

Chapter 40

AFTER TAKING WHAT must have been the quickest of baths, Malin dressed and headed out the door. Despite the drizzle the weather forecaster had warned would become something stronger, he chose to wear the black jacket meant for summer. He chose it because Amy had always liked it, and he left full of promise.

Heading into the city centre, he allowed himself a furtive glance through the glass front of Organico and was not surprised that the last employee to have served him there was not to be seen. He shrugged his shoulders and told himself it didn't bother him, not now.

Nearing what he had always viewed as being the 'main' bus terminal, he ventured within the local Forbidden Planet store for the first time in months. He recognised the staff and could have easily exchanged pleasantries, but he did not know their names. At The Drive In played across the store speakers, but he didn't recognise many of their songs. The layout of the store, however, was comfortingly familiar. He welcomed the surprise of seeing 2000AD alongside a few other titles. He hadn't given the title a second thought in years and was happy to see it was still going.

He stopped at a new display. A thick, hardback book, an omnibus on the work of Jake Mayer. Malin didn't recognise the name, nor the photograph of the youngish, uncomfortable-looking figure gracing the cover, yet he found his hand reaching out toward it and couldn't explain why. Consciously aware of his actions, he smiled as if in respect for the deceased, turned and made his way to the collection of *Pop! Vinyl* figurines against the far wall.

Amy had always been a fan of The Addams Family and, knowing there was a fairly new animated film, he hoped to find a figurine of one of the characters for her. Of course, he didn't – no matter how long he examined the display. In the end he admitted defeat and left the store, handing a *Big Issue* seller some money but not insisting on taking a magazine. He told himself it was his good deed. Really, he wanted to purchase a little good karma.

Malin boarded the bus, took a complimentary Metro newspaper from the front and found a seat with ease. The journey began. He moved to the horoscopes section and read his own for that day. He didn't believe in these; at least he wasn't willing to admit to himself that he may, he simply wanted words of encouragement – words that this was going to go how he wanted it.

He checked his wristwatch as his stop approached. It was already nearing lunch time. He became excited at the idea of taking Amy to a local café or even the McDonald's for lunch. Then it dawned on him. She worked as a library assistant. What if the library were closed due to government cuts?

He tried to calm himself, told himself it would all come down to fate. And still, when he stepped off the bus, it wasn't the heavy rain that had him walking so quickly.

He stopped at the traffic lights facing the old

redbrick building. The doors were open wide despite the weather, and lights were behind the windows. The library was open. And he realised how he must look, standing soaking wet, and allowed himself to chuckle. He would walk in and make a grand statement, and–

Amy came hurrying out of the door, pulling her grey coat close, and his heart stopped. She hadn't seen him, but he could see the look on her face, and he smiled at how she clearly wasn't looking forward to going out in *this* weather. He put his first step forward and stopped as someone came running into sight, out from behind a work van. A tall man in a padded coat. He saw the change of expression on Amy's face. Saw how happy she was as she planted a kiss against his lips before she linked her arm through his and the two walked on, blissfully unaware they were being observed.

Chapter 41

HE WALKED BACK into the city. He walked through the heart, making his way towards the docks. Malin knew a lot of office workers used the newer buildings, and he knew the older buildings attracted their share of tourists, but he hoped the downfall would prevent him from seeing many of either group.

He hoped to simply drop into the water and allow it to take him anywhere, as long as it was far from here.

But he noticed the payphone near the black painted railings he had come to, black railings covered in padlocks fastened by the young and in love. He wondered if, in this day and age, the payphone worked or if it had been left as some historical monument.

The glass that hadn't been kicked through was covered by deep scratches and carved names. Inside, the floor was wet with what may have been urine, the shelf to place coins ready to be used holding a can of White Ace.

Malin lifted the receiver, placed it against his ear and heard the dial tone.

The card Marcus had given him was tucked inside his wallet.

Malin made a call for reverse charges, spoke his name when he was asked to and waited patiently as an automated voice told him contact was being made with the number he had read out. Of course, he expected it to go unanswered.

"Mr Malin," Marcus spoke cheerily as he came on

the line, "how can I help you?"

"My dead sister-in-law told me my stepbrother's soul isn't with her," he said, "it's in the possession of a jinn."

"Well," Marcus said, "let us see what we can do about that…"

EPILOGUE

LOREN TRACEY JUMPED off the bus and was hurrying down Redford Street West before the driver had restarted his route.

It wasn't yet six o'clock in the morning and Loren was in a poverty-stricken area. Signs made claims that the area was undergoing regeneration, but there was nothing to show that this was true. All the council had really done was paint bright and colourful patterns over the boards covering the doors and windows of long abandoned houses; some with rooftops that had been left damaged following acts of arson.

It hadn't always been as such.

Cobbled streets and Georgian houses.

A lifetime ago, this place had been inhabited by the wealthy. As times changed, the homes were brought and cheaply turned into flats. As properties became empty, they were claimed by the destitute and, once this was underway, it was only those entirely out of luck or students with no prior knowledge of the area that were drawn to the premises.

Burglaries occurred often to fund a number of vile habits, and prostitution was rife.

Loren held no empathy for those unfortunates left dwelling here. She coloured her hair a vibrant orange with intentions of drawing attention. She wanted them to notice the hair, then imagine how much her expensive suit cost – to wonder if the designer handbag she carried was authentic (it was). Of course, the expensive attire was, for her, to draw attention from her otherwise vulgar appearance. Her plump and pale skin always appeared greasy, no matter how often she bathed, and her teeth were almost as those of an infant, though greatly discoloured and unnaturally sharp. But it was her feet she greatly disliked, no matter how expensive the shoes she slipped them into. Loren's feet were noticeably small. So small, in fact, that the running joke through high school and college was that she didn't have feet, she had trotters.

She turned at the corner of Redford Street West, the old post box signalling the start of Vining Road. Hurrying on through the early morning cold, she told herself that she was almost there.

A milkman had parked his float a matter of feet in front of her. Loren wondered how she had overlooked it until now. She couldn't even remember the last time she had seen a milkman; she was certain everybody nipped to the supermarket or corner store for their milk, nowadays.

The milkman looked young, probably no older than nineteen. Thin, with bright pimples across his cheeks. He noticed her as he was collecting a few bottles from the back of his vehicle. Bottles that would be placed on doorsteps and most likely stolen by passing drunks, or having their caps removed by seagulls.

"Morning, love," the lad smiled.

Loren looked at him with contempt; pulled her handbag a little closer and even increased her pace. She found herself wondering, again, why he looked so young. An apprentice, maybe? Did they have apprentice milkmen?

She noticed the vomit on the pavement with but a moment to spare and managed to avoid stepping in it. It looked to be in the process of congealing; was a bright, almost neon colour, and containing what she assumed to have been fried rice.

Loren turned at the last corner, onto Knight Street. She shook the mental image of the puddle of vomit from her mind and wondered just how, exactly, people of such low class could share space with such tremendous power.

Each front door on Knight Street had a minimum of three mailboxes and three doorbells. Each door, with the exception of that for number 12. Number 12 had neither a mailbox nor a doorbell. It did, however, have a large brass knocker.

Loren ascended the two stone steps to the door and knocked loudly. Standing beside the living room window, she saw how stained the net curtains were despite there being no light on within.

The light would not come on until she was inside. That was now a part of the routine.

Certain the required time had passed, Loren reached into her handbag and pushed the three, A4 Manila envelopes aside to reach the mortice key behind them. She used this to unlock the door to 12 Knight Street. The pungent smell that she knew all too well felt to race out of the house to greet her. Undeterred, she stepped inside and closed the door shut behind her. Once she had bolted the door, a table lamp was turned on in the nearest room.

Like clockwork.

Loren straightened her posture, tidied her hair as

best she could without use of a mirror, and strode into the room. The smell was at its worst here; Loren was sure of that. And it wasn't the damp or the mould that was responsible for the stench, but the figure sitting at the small table before the closed blackout curtains in an otherwise unfurnished room.

The man was ghastly pale and wearing what had been brown trousers, a very long time ago. His hair was long, greasy and matted, as was his beard and his slender hands looked to be covered in the dirt of disturbed graves.

Heterochromia had given the man one green eye and one brown.

For a while, the two simply stared to one another. Loren *knew* something far worse may have been upstairs, but the broken wretch before her still caused her to feel unease.

At last, the silent figure gave something of a nod; lifted his right hand from his knee and gestured for her to come closer.

"I have three files for you, as promised," Loren said, approaching the table, clammy hands already pulling the Manila envelopes from her handbag. "Even I'm impressed by the level of research."

She smiled, almost bowed and held the envelopes out to be taken – a moment in which she *always* feared the silent figure would reach out at lightning speed and take a hold of her wrist.

Of course, he never did. His eyes briefly fell to the table before moving back onto her.

"As you insist," she smiled and carefully dropped the envelopes atop of the dusty table.

Her heart leaped to the back of her throat a moment later as loud, thundering footsteps moved overhead. They sounded to have started directly above her and moved towards the door she had entered. Instinctively, Loren looked upward and was horrified to see how a patch of damp or mould upon the ceiling seemed to come alive and follow the sound of each step.

And what would she do if those same footsteps came down the stairs, one step at a time? Would she try to run? Would she scream, or would terror render her silent?

But the steps ceased and, as silence reclaimed the room, the swirling pattern of decay upon the ceiling became still once more. Relieved, she brought her gaze down and found the eyes of the wretched, pitiful figure had not strayed from her. And for a moment he simply stared a moment longer before giving a solitary nod of the head, his hand already reaching for the switch of the table lamp. Loren smiled, felt she may have said something along the lines of how the pleasure was hers but wasn't entirely sure, and made her way back to the front door.

She managed to have the bolt back a moment before the light of the table lamp was extinguished. Loren hurriedly pulled the door open and stepped out onto the cold street, pulling the door shut behind her. She crossed the street, placing distance between her and the house as quickly as she could manage, and took a discreet glance towards the upper windows. Of course, she saw nothing looking back at her.

Almost twenty-four hours later, the shattered remains of a man whom Loren had given the three envelopes to, made his way through the darkness of the house. He entered the kitchen and tossed two folders into the kitchen sink; took the bottle of lighter fluid from the worktop and splashed it over the papers. Finally, he took a match from the windowsill and struck it against the wall. The flame was as a flare within the darkened room. The walls, almost alive with cockroaches, became a great mess of activity.

But he paid no heed to such things. Once he knew the flame was strong, he calmly dropped the match atop of the papers and watched them burn, the spreading of crumpling ash going from brown to black to grey underneath a dazzling yellow being almost hypnotic to him.

One file, of course, had not been destroyed... Not yet. The file remained upstairs, now out of his touch.

The surviving file focused entirely on Kelley Stranack.

THE END

Thanks for reading!
We hope you enjoyed this book.
If you did then please consider leaving a review at
Amazon – it would mean a lot to us all.

MORE FROM
sci-fi-cafe

Available to buy in paperback and eBook from
Amazon and other good online stores.
Scan the affiliate links in the QR codes to find out
more about each book.

Look out for our Audiobooks on
Audible and Amazon too

Transplant
Greenways
The Tribe
The Seed Garden

The Threads Which Bind us

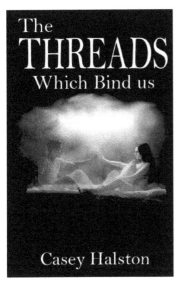

Anna's life is falling apart. She's skipping college, lost touch with her friends and can't face her family. She wakes late to find the ghost of a young man in her room. He has no memory of his past life nor any clue as to why he has appeared here.

In the beginning, she fights to get rid of him, but something about his glasslike sensuality fascinates her as he is drawn towards the only person in his world that can hear him, see him, *touch* him.

As they work to find out who he is, how he died and what is keeping him in the realm of the living, Anna's own recent and tragic past surfaces.

Content advisory: Mild sex references, suicide references. Alcohol.

ISBN: 978-1-910779-98-9

The Wolf Inside Us

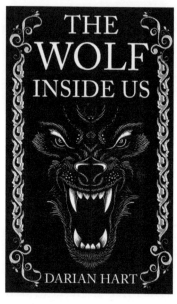

Jake is a reclusive genius shut away in his penthouse apartment where he draws his award winning zombie comics. Kat is one of his biggest fans. She's also his publisher's office manager and each week gets to visit Jake to see his latest work.

Over the years, Kat has developed a soft spot for Jake, so it's not surprising that she's completely thrown when he suddenly disappears. But stranger still, why did he leave a tiny puppy behind, all alone, and where did he get it?

Kat's relationship grows from more than simple puppy love in this sensual werewolf romance where life throws all it has at this girl and her dog.

Content advisory: Mild sex and fantasy sex references, alcohol, mild fantasy violence.

ISBN 978-1-910779-97-2

The Girl from the Temple Ruins

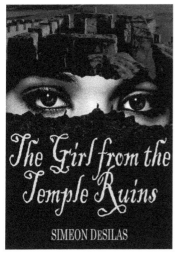

A temple to the goddess Amalishah lies in the remotest wastelands of Assyria. She is their protector but to others she is known as The Monster.

The Hittite prince Artaxias visits the Palace of the Goddess to implore the temple priests to free prisoners captured from the border. He knows their fate, the appalling human sacrifice that will be made to the goddess who must feed on human blood.

Four thousand years have eroded the memory and the evidence of these events until British archaeologist Michael Townsend discovers the subterranean lair of the goddess. Michael is visited and instantly captivated by a mysterious and beautiful woman. The Hittites called her monster, a creature now called vampire.

ISBN: 978-1910779-41-5

City of Storms

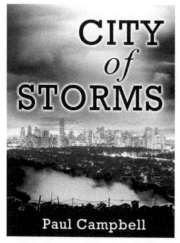

When top foreign correspondent Sean Brian flies into Manila in the Philippines, a typhoon and a political revolution are uppermost in his thoughts.

But what also awaits will turn his already busy life into a roller coaster of romance, adventure, elation and despair.

At the centre of this transformation is an infant boy child, born, abandoned and plunged into street poverty in the grim underbelly of an Asian metropolis.

This is the catalyst for a story ranging from the corrupt, violent world of back street city sex clubs and drug addiction, to the clean air of the Sulu Sea and the South Pacific; from the calm safety of an island paradise to the violent guerilla world of the notorious Golden Triangle and the southern Philippines archipelago.

As we follow the child, Bagyo, into fledgling manhood, we can only wonder at the ripples that spread from one individual to engulf so many others – and at the injustice that still corrodes life on the mean streets of the world.

ISBN: 978-1908387-99-8